AGES APART

AGES APART

Enrico Palandri

Translated from the Italian by
F. O'Donnell

COLLINS HARVILL
8 Grafton Street, London W1
1989

COLLINS HARVILL
William Collins Sons & Co. Ltd
London · Glasgow · Sydney · Auckland
Toronto · Johannesburg

BRITISH LIBRARY CATALOGUING IN PUBLICATION DATA

Palandri, Enrico
Ages apart.
I. Title   II. Le Pietre e il sale. *English*
853'.914   PQ4876.A383

ISBN 0 00 271461 2

First published in Italy by Garzanti Editore S.p.A., Milan,
in 1986 under the title *Le Pietre e il Sale*
First published in Great Britain by Collins Harvill 1989

Copyright © Garzanti Editore S.p.A., 1986
Translation copyright © William Collins Sons & Co. Ltd 1989

Photoset in Linotron Bembo by
Rowland Phototypesetting Ltd, Bury St Edmunds, Suffolk
Printed and bound in Great Britain by
Hartnolls Ltd, Bodmin, Cornwall

To Venice

ONE

Donne cortesi, e belle
Che di luce amorosa
Gli occhi appagate, e accendete i cori
Quasi lucide stelle
In questa notte ombrosa,
Sgombrate voi le tenebre, e gli horrori.

TORQUATO TASSO

I

After missing what may have been the last of the few ferries across the Giudecca, Marco Ivancich walked slowly along the Fondamenta delle Zitelle, gazing at the stars. It was a late summer night; the breeze was blowing softly over the lagoon; it played on his face and hair and seemed to open a hole in the heat. These fresh, invisible caresses brought him relief; he liked to detect in them the friendly hand of solitude, ever ready to scoop him up, even out of these tiny failures. He watched the ferry cross the canal, and then turned back to the stars.

He imagined the silence; it seemed to him that thoughts lay hidden among the dark folds of the night: the waves, the clouds, the shadows. The sky was empty and, had not gravity held him firmly to the ground, the speed of the rotating globe, or indeed his slightest movement would have flung him into the infinite, all alone for an immeasurable distance. He imagined not dying, not ever being able to die, resisting hunger and thirst and every other need. He imagined an end to feet and hands and breath; the eyes, however, remained open and watched as planets, meteorites, entire galaxies were spun away with him to be lost in the void, fragments hurled in different directions by an explosion. He imagined having no mouth left to scream with, but no fear left either. His ears, too, remained alert, forced to listen to the invading silence and miss not a syllable.

He would need no sleep, ignore weariness; no distraction would be left to spare his consciousness: his vigil would know no pause nor ending. As he followed the imaginary trajectory of that fall through the sky, he thought for a moment that he was dead. Then he became aware of the movement of the water, the sound of the waves lapping against the stone steps of the quay: no, he was not dead, he had merely gone missing for a moment.

His eyes turned back to the stars, and he drew a thin stream of air through his nostrils. He held his breath for a few moments and felt himself at long last prepared for his stellar voyage. Then the need for air forced him to draw another breath, just as pain forces a cry; but pain and need had already disappeared; perhaps it was just his imagination again and nothing had happened. Like seagulls in search of food, his eyes now skimmed over the surface of the water, following the reflection of a light to the shore opposite. A streetlamp, tall and solitary, broke the long naked line of the Zattere, and it seemed to him that all his thoughts now settled upon it, exhausted by their race across the reflections on the water. Marco watched the rhythmic kiss of the water and the stone, the flow of the tide and felt exhausted, like a shipwrecked man who has no hope but goes on swimming until his strength is all gone, until the sea, whose surface he barely cleaves, swallows him in its depths.

But his legs bore him on, took him through the odours and the dim radiance of the occasional streetlamps, to brush past dreams, memories, enchantment, a total surrender. Another ferry came. Marco boarded it and stood on the prow to feel the breeze; as he gazed over the bulwarks at the water he pondered in his heart, how foolish it was as it pierced him from within and denied the comfort of mere levity. One by one he pictured the alleys, the squares, the bridges which separated him from home and the mere thought of the distance yet to cover exhausted him. He wondered at the stupidity of imagining that he could die in such a way, but his thoughts were still too contradictory and forbade him the detachment he longed for; and again, like a sudden violent pain, the sense of his own failure, of his inadequacy, of being hamstrung by his own ambiguities and the ineptitude, these and countless other thoughts, every whit as agonizing and nameless, set upon him like hounds which had tasted the blood of their prey and now pursued all the more relentlessly. Just as the hunted beast looks steadfastly ahead, this being the only direction where death is not a certainty, Marco looked out on the water and to the shore beyond, his eyes seeking to avoid tears, as he searched ahead of him for some fragment of reality beyond reach of that hunt of which he was the quarry.

Suddenly he thought he saw a figure slip into an alley: men are alive, he thought, and the seaweed and the fish, and felt tacitly grateful to his own heart for allowing him that moment's respite.

It was almost morning when he got home. Dawn was breaking over the rooftops towards the east, spreading across the whole arc of the sky. Against what was still the palest blue, the dark outlines of the buildings in Campo San Polo appeared like giants fallen asleep around a spent fire. Marco carried a chair to the window overlooking the square and sat down to breathe in the morning and listen to its sounds: the opening of shutters, ageless women leaning out to greet the day after their night's rest. Someone hurried across the flagstones at the far end of the square and the echoing footsteps died away between the walls of the narrow alleys. And the calls of the birds already converging from every quarter, the wondrous spirallings of the younger ones, while their elders floated in the sky alone, still full of sleep, planing from cloud down to rooftop and, with a single beat of the wing, back up again.

13

They are flying south, thought Marco, now that autumn is coming, and with a flight of that same imagination which forever condemned him to gulp down the next breath, he laid his sorrows on a swallow's back and felt the weight lift from him. He slid into bed and spent a long time lying there with his eyes open, wandering outside the window among the clouds and electric wires stretched across the square, until the city was awake and the daytime noises played on him like a gentle, endless lullaby, putting him to sleep.

When he awoke some hours later, he felt calm and fearless. One by one, his thoughts detached themselves and rose out of bed, turning straight away towards the thousand things to be done, falling into an ordered line as they organized the day ahead. He lay there observing the bustling activity of his mind and marvelled at it: he would get to work on a translation that he had abandoned months ago, then he'd phone the landlady to complain about the damp patch on the ceiling; he might even buy a newspaper. But these intentions lasted only a moment; he watched them burst like soap bubbles in the smoke of his first cigarette, leaving only a blob on the floor. Outside the sun was shining, the day was alive, full of men and things; the shrill voices of children and the murmur of adults reached his ears from the square below. He half shut his eyes as if this would help him not to hear. He would have liked to ask himself some questions, to pursue the speculations abandoned the night before, but diffidence and a strange fear had enveloped his heart in a morbid silence; he was left once again only with inexplicable, disjointed colours and movements. The softness and warmth of his nest were gone, yet still he could not rise from his bed. He would wait for evening. He searched for some handhold, cranny or crack through which he could vent his thoughts, but found no certainty even in the walls; light, smoke, voices, shreds of reality without context.

Thus life flew away, like a sigh, in the closed sky of that room. He wanted to die, wanted it desperately and soon, to deliver himself from the vigil he had mounted over his own decay; for his conscience's sake he would have liked to lay out the cards of past events once more, like in a game of patience, and this time force it to a solution. Yet death did not seem to him in any way an ending, it was merely weariness.

It was evening again, the end of another wasted day. He hadn't succeeded in doing anything, he hadn't looked at the blue of the sky, nor seen the sun: sleep had brought him no rest and he had burnt himself up in an aching emptiness; this grieved him enormously, and forced him, just as in his imaginary suicide, to take another breath, to devour the next moment. Like every evening for the past few months his home seemed a very hell to him; it forced him out on the streets in search of a beauty in which he did not believe and which would anyway have eluded him. He grabbed his cigarettes and jacket and hurried out, as if the emptiness at his shoulders clutched at him and, like Lot, he could have made his escape only on one condition. The doorway, the stairs, the street door, the alley, walls, the quiet water and there, finally, the sky! Far away, up there among the stars he would have felt perfectly at ease, in the freezing cold and absolute darkness that doesn't fear dawn's approach; but among the warm bodies of men and animals, in the torture of living blood, of the rhythm of nature, of things which destroy themselves, devour each other and putrefy, where every smell is an outrage and every colour an assault, down here on the accursed earth of life, one can only die. He was breathing calmly, but encountering the first passers-by wounded him. For a while he took refuge in his thoughts, then, forcing a passage through his throat, he asked somebody for a match.

2

It was only in darkness and silence that Marco did not feel like a prisoner. The crazy blue of the sky, the shriek of the sun drowning in the sea bound him so firmly to his emotions that he felt chained to them. Every second, while daylight gave a shape to things, he burnt up a lifetime, from birth to death. Hope was born in the opening of a flower in the morning, in the smile of a stranger, in all that could be done to make the world a better place, and died in disappointment because the flower would fade, the stranger remain a stranger, the world would stay the same as ever.

In his torment he recognized the danger of a mental breakdown, but also the condition his sensibility needed in order to survive. He could no longer ignore everything that happened, even right before his eyes; the link which day had established with him was so strong that all he could do in the end was avoid it.

The evening, on the other hand, he welcomed; he welcomed the hours when his footsteps and his thoughts ran free, from past memories to the future, from what lay close around him to what was beyond reach.

He had sat down to smoke a cigarette on the steps of a house behind the Tolentini, and was gazing at a scrap of starry sky framed by the shapes of the houses, and listening to people's footsteps coming and going past the point where the steps gave on to the fondamenta, when two young people stopped right there on the steps.

"Let's have another kiss, Nina, then tell me to go."

"Come on, come on up, love. There's no risk – honest! My parents sleep like logs."

"Yes, but if your father does get up he'll shoot me."

"But he won't get up. I wouldn't ask you otherwise."

Suddenly Marco found them right in front of him – their two ages put together would have made up his own. He thought he ought to move to let them by, but instead he stayed still, blocking their way.

"Do you live here?" he asked.

"Yes, I live here. Why?" answered the girl.

"I heard what you were saying. If you like you can make love at my flat."

The boy's face broke into a broad smile of agreement, he was so relieved to be spared the challenge the girl had set him. She made no move, however, and Marco feared that she would be suspicious of his offer and refuse it.

"I'm Marco," he said, getting to his feet. The boy, now completely won over, as if the name was some kind of infallible guarantee, held out his hand.

"My name's Luca."

"And you're Nina."

"How ever do you know?" asked Luca in amazement.

Nina instantly remembered that Luca had called her by name a moment ago, and gave a sort of affirmative grunt, though remaining on her guard.

They set off towards Marco's flat, Nina and Luca holding hands and somewhat keeping their distance. Hooking off to sleep in a stranger's house and without permission was totally against the rules. They were talking it over in whispers, trying not to be heard: "He's not a stranger, he's called Marco" – "Anyway, they'd never say yes." This was the

17

first time they would have spent the whole night together and they were excited.

Marco gave them his bed and went to sleep on the sofa. In the morning he made coffee and took them some in their room:

"Did you sleep well?"

"Yes, it's a lovely bed," said Luca, sitting up.

Nina was lying on her side, half asleep. Catching a whiff of the coffee, she felt around with one hand for the cup then propped herself up on an elbow and began to sip, her eyes still shut. The nipples of her delicate breasts stood out like two seeds popping from the fruit. Marco felt a desire to caress them, to kiss them; he reached over and brushed them lightly with one finger. In a sharp, instinctive movement, Nina covered her breasts, spilling the coffee on the sheet. Marco drew back his hand with an almost identical movement. His had been but an unthinking gesture, but now he felt like an intruder, on Nina, on Luca, on himself, an intruder in his own house.

"I'm going out to buy the paper. That way you'll have the chance to get up and get out from under my feet." His voice was angrier than he really meant it to be – Nina's reaction seemed like another of those bloodhounds that hunted him down at night. "But why?" he thought, as he saw her own frightened eyes questioning him: "What's the matter? What d'you mean?"

"Why? Everything has been so natural until now: what you said to each other, your kisses, my invitation, the lazy way you reached for the coffee-cup in your sleep." But Marco said none of this. He stood before their two young bodies immersed in the illusions of love, almost compulsory at their age, and they seemed to him so naked and defenceless, waiting for the massacre of life that would pass a thousand hands over those breasts, kiss those lips a thousand times, only with more dishonesty, and under God knows what false pretences. But what can kids know of such things? Poor children, so entangled in love! Marco's face expressed these thoughts, one by one, but he gave no words to them. His voice had vanished into a black hole in his throat and was fighting with a lump of things to say and not to say, fighting to defend himself, or them, or both, and the entire world, to overcome that silence and repair the thread of understanding which his gesture had broken. Motionless, Nina watched him as he searched the dumb air between those walls for something to say. Finally Marco cut the knot with a distrait gesture not unmixed with pity, and shrugged off his thoughtless action. He let his body relax from the tension which had held the two nailed to the bed, passing a hand through his hair and heaving a slow, deep sigh, which put the youngsters at their ease. Then he left the house.

Luca stared at Nina with eyes full of amusement and round as moons.

"He's mad."

In Marco's look she saw herself as ageless, stripped to the bone; she saw herself as she would always be, as she had always been; she gazed into those moon-eyes that looked at her face from the enchanted garden of their youth, from the love-games they had shared until a few moments ago. His eyes, she saw, remained unaware of all that had happened to her. She suddenly felt divided from those eyes by an intangible distance, and looked at them from afar as from another planet, trying with all her strength to draw them to her. She tried to speak, to utter a cry which could reach him across the void, but all that came out was a strange bleat which made Luca laugh. So, disconcerted, she gazed at a damp-stain on the ceiling. She imagined that now at school they were calling her name, "Nina Contin". She had to stand up, leave her desk and answer questions.

Luca got up, happy as a sparrow among crumbs left for him on the window-sill, and began a little dance of kisses and toothpaste, of chatter and jokes from the bathroom. He even hummed a tune. Nina remained gripped by that damp-stain for an age; thoughts, many and incomprehensible, passed through her in every direction, from head to foot, to her belly and away, out of the window, back home, to school, to the sea.

"Hey, aren't you going to get dressed? Get a move on, Nina, before he gets back and chews us out. We can have our breakfast in the square and meet the others at school."

Nina slipped out of bed, and found to her delight that it was not difficult to get up. She hugged Luca, her friend, her loved one, who had not noticed the strange mood which had come over her that morning; nor would she ever have tried to describe it to him. She pulled on her trousers and sweater and gave him another hug. This second embrace was almost to prove that she was still a young girl, that embracing Luca was simple and beautiful, as it had always been. But even as she hugged him she was aware of thinking these things, and when he bent down to kiss her lips, Nina buried her head in his shoulder, fearing he might read in her face all the strange thoughts that had come to her that morning.

"Let's go," she said firmly, forcing herself to swallow her confusion. Luca had already run downstairs while she was putting on her shoes. Before leaving she made a round of the house, drinking in every detail, and it seemed as if the things she saw were taking their places one by one in the depths of her mind. She went into the little study where Marco had slept; the cushions on the sofa still bore the imprint of his body. She touched the spines of the books in the same unthinking way in which, returning home alone, she ran her finger along the bars of gates. There was half a page inserted in the typewriter, and a great muddle of papers all over the desk. To the half-page she added: "Forgive me if I hurt you, Marco, I didn't mean to." Then she ran down the stairs to Luca, pursuing that girlhood of which she had for the first time become aware, and which she had felt sliding away from her.

In front of the news-stand Marco completely reassumed the character he had so often impersonated on waking up in the morning, anxious to start a new life in which work and commitment would fully occupy him, and prevent him staying out all night. Without a moment's hesitation he bought a daily paper and went into the café, ordered a *cappuccino* and got out his cigarettes. These habits which had once enabled him to live almost painlessly, slipping from one day into the next – just as the reports in that paper slipped from one country to another, from one era to the next on the planet Earth, without touching them at all – these habits made up the repertoire of gestures and thoughts which he had abandoned. Just as an actor rehearsing a part studies the inner meaning of every stress and every movement, so Marco observed, without a trace of irony or malice, how others lived in this world, and then repeated the same gestures to see if they would work for him too. What the newsagent thought of him or his work, or of life, had to be a matter of total indifference to him. He didn't have to smile at the man, or be specially nice to him, everything would be perfectly all right: he would be given the paper, though he had to remember to pay for it. And he would sit down in the café like everybody else. Everything had gone perfectly, and in fact here he was reading his paper, or on the point of doing so, with his cup of coffee, a cigarette poised between his fingers ready to be smoked. He would have liked to have shared his success with some other human being, but that would have meant explaining what it amounted to, which was more than Marco could cope with, so on the whole he felt better off as he was, on his own.

He started to peruse the paper: the number of things that had happened that morning was beyond belief. It seemed to him that they were perfectly right to print such enormous headlines, although none of the articles which followed managed to keep up the tone and the drama promised by the huge lettering. For example, he read: SPAIN MUST BE PART OF EUROPE, an opinion with which he heartily agreed, and one which he had never had occasion to doubt. Marco looked through the article to see if he could discover the identity of this eccentric, this doubting Thomas, but unfortunately there was no mention of him, nor any reason given to explain the necessity for the statement. He'd have to find out from some other source, he thought, and passed on to the next item of news, also featured on the front page. Several footballers were shown embracing ecstatically, and the caption informed him that TURIN BEATEN ON HOME GROUND BY THE NEWCOMERS COMO. To have put this on the same page as an article which questioned Spain's place in Europe seemed a little exaggerated. However, it was a good photograph – those footballers seemed so happy they made Marco smile to himself and think: "This editor must be a philanthropist." He then saw that at least twelve pages were dedicated to the same sport, and thought: "This editor must be mad," or, on second thoughts, "I'm mad myself." But it was the crime page that really sent shivers down his spine. The horrible goings-on described in merciless detail with a sort of light abandon, with cynicism in fact, and the morbid prying into other people's business seemed like a disgusting morsel thrown down for some wild beast. Who can swallow such muck? Who can bear to see the misery of others exploited like this?

He went home, tidied his desk, sat down at the typewriter and re-read the half-page he had left in it. When he came to the couple of lines Nina had written, he angrily tore out the sheet. So that small-breasted, tongue-tied girl had a heart after all? Marco was not touched, nor was he really surprised. At that age one is scarcely aware that saying "I didn't mean to" is meaningless. Now he would have to retype that half-page. "I didn't mean to" indeed! "Who did mean to, then?"

He set to work and thought no more about her.

3

Marco had been in Venice only a few months. A friend had handed on a small apartment with a blocked rent, which enabled him to gather together the bits and pieces he had collected over the last years and left with friends in one city and another. He had never been able to consider himself well off. He did translations for a publisher who paid him poorly and sporadically; or else he wrote articles for a newspaper which survived only on subscriptions and was worse off than he was. Now that a roving way of life no longer forced him to keep abandoning his routine and then struggling to piece it together again, he hoped to get down to some more serious projects in his new home.

After his encounter with Luca and Nina, he settled peaceably down to work for a while, and as soon as he felt that he had enough money he also felt the need for company, the presence of other human beings. He began to frequent the Serafini, a café patronized by a small circle of local intellectuals – schoolteachers, critics, artists who swapped hackneyed tired commonplaces, as one would expect, decking them out in the borrowed plumage of some bright new line in philosophy – but my dear, it's the *dernier cri*! – all bursting to establish their group's role in the evolution of western culture. The continuous squabbles between the followers of fashion and the avant-garde, between ideologists and self-seekers, between the old and the new, tended to cast a pall of tedium over the conversation, but, as in every group, the real catalyst was something else: the love affairs, the betrayals, the friendships. Each member of the group followed the doings of his comrades with a morbid curiosity counterbalanced, however, by a total lack of interest in outsiders. All they knew about the other inhabitants of the city was that they belonged to some other group which was the target of a whole catalogue of unflattering and derisive opinions, as superficial as they were groundless. About the world outside they possessed only the vaguest notion. Such ignorance, far from denting the group's boundless self-importance, enabled any member who spent a few weeks in Rome, say, or Kenya, to dumbfound his comrades with fantastic and unlikely tales about what went on in those other worlds. These were necessarily a mere extrapolation from the one little world they knew, and tended to confirm them in the view – which they never seriously challenged – that this was the most beautiful city in the world, and absolutely the only place to live, especially as they, the cream of the city's intelligentsia, had managed here to form a group. As we follow the fortunes of Luca and Nina we shall see, on the other hand, that the youngsters of Venice often felt that life would only be possible away from the island. Their walks would take them down to the port, to watch the ships and dream of far-off countries, of other possible worlds, and there, on the threshold of youth, they spoke of almost nothing but leaving Venice.

But every group, however diverse its ambitions, was ultimately united in a single collective notion, of different application to each generation or class but nonetheless common to all: a notion which stood above all debate, uniting grandmother and grandchild, countess and gondolier, across the barrier of conflict to stand shoulder to shoulder against "the outsider". This notion could be indulged in to various degrees depending on how far a person was inclined to stick his nose into other people's affairs, and of course on the place he held in this society, but nobody, not even nature's hermits, could stand aside from it altogether. Nina's grandmother, for example, on meeting someone for the first time, established straight off who his parents or grandparents were and where they lived, bandying names about until a common acquaintance came to light, or at the very least a name familiar to both parties. Then, with a happy smile which seemed to say, "Ah, so you too belong to the planet Earth?" or something equally extraordinary, she relaxed and sank back in her armchair with a long sigh of satisfaction. After a brief pause she would add some commonplace such as "He was the son of my godmother Bepina's cousin" – or of some gondolier, or of the town councillor, or of the priest, or of whoever else, known to her only by name.

Even if the old stories were dying along with the old people, the way of telling them, of setting out the sequence of events, differed only slightly from ancient tradition, and managed to cross the class barriers where nothing else could do so. The "patois" penetrated those aristocratic walls and seeped out again through the tradesman's entrance or through some prodigal son, finding its way back into the city and the great communal fable.

A story passed on by word of mouth is subject to rules and limits far more tightly drawn than those governing a written story – a book can be abandoned, condensed, rewritten. The tale of a city can never be read in its entirety; it wraps us in its myths, it absorbs us in its metabolism. Only in special circumstances, in some crisis, can one of the countless narrators throw some light on the rhythms and pick out the framework, the skeleton of the story. The whole community may be struck dumb, unable to speak about some event which has cut too deeply into the moral well-being of the city. Madness, crime, generosity, erotic passion, these all lie outside the ethos of an oral tradition, and the only relationship which the community may establish with such situations is one of exorcism. Thus, if it happened that mention could no longer be made of certain people because the circumstances of their lives placed them outside the scope of normal gossip, one amused oneself inventing slanders which fairly stifled any lingering affection one might have felt for them, even in the rather sterile and anonymous form of group affection, and banished them from mind. At a deeper level, it was sometimes the patois itself which, like an organism, rejected anything intensely felt, anything complicated or simply too bizarre to be woven into the general saga. Common sense, confined by rigid, inscrutable taboos, would propagate itself like an indigenous plant that grows everywhere, in places where it has been cultivated and in places where fire has razed all vegetation.

Even the little group of intellectuals with whom Marco associated was a direct descendant of this ancient, abstruse nucleus, in which linguistic homogeneity was the last recognizable vestige. Thus Marco too – he had after all been seen wandering about at night, but above all he was *foresto*, an outsider – had been adorned with a garland of anecdotes and jibes, which made his presence in the café at this point slightly embarrassing.

His admission to the group came about slowly. None of them had sufficient reason to persist in being hostile, but they all needed a while to get the poison out of their system before they could include him in their discussions. Marco felt vaguely uncomfortable about the reverential and slightly awestruck manner in which they spoke about literature, and also about the fact that they spoke of it so frequently. They were like a class of high-school students who have been goaded by an intransigent schoolmaster into studying, understanding, indeed loving literature and who therefore cannot but hate and shun it and totally misunderstand it; they offered timid, run-of-the-mill opinions, oppressed as they were by a common, Damoclean nightmare: to be caught on the wrong foot, snubbed by the rest and sent to Coventry. At least half of them were destined to become one of those very same teachers who had made their lives a misery in their 'teens, to no purpose. Their contempt for the models which they were destined to reincarnate made it all the harder for them to understand how the promises of youth could have been so fickle as to abandon them to that profession. So they wore a typical air of suppressed rebellion, all frustrated and distorted, ready to catch fire from the first intellectual novelty they met.

Marco, who didn't credit himself with any exceptional talents that might snatch him away from the daily round and the labour of earning his own bread, learnt to live on the fringe of this common exchange, studied the dialect as a foreign language and, as far as he could, suspended judgment on his associates. His ability as a conversationalist – he knew how to make connections between things and carry his listeners into a world that appeared new and different – drew from the depths of the group those rebellious aspirations which caused each one of them to yearn for a world remade from scratch, with themselves occupying a better place in their career and, above all, in the opinion of their fellow-citizens. This side-effect of his conversation didn't much please Marco, because it was a misunderstanding. The use he made, for example, of reasoning through paradox was purely a literary device, and the political interpretation given to his argument by the others often distorted his own meaning, forcing him to explain himself in words of one syllable, and carefully to avoid any hint of metaphor, which could leave him charged with nebulous ideologies, or worse, with being accomplice to nameless clandestine organizations.

After a few weeks the initiation was complete. His arrival in the café started to become the occasion for exaggerated compliments, the quotation of some expression of his, and the group seemed to make room for him, to put their relationship on a firmer footing. Thus it happened that Marina Dondini, meeting him in the street one afternoon, slipped her arm into his and began telling him everything they'd said of him behind his back before he had been accepted. It didn't even enter Marina's head that these gratuitous speculations might be painful to Marco; instead she seemed confident of winning his trust by naming the author of each slanderous story and the trivial pretexts which had occasioned it. When she'd finished with the gossip, she asked him who he really was, and to Marco this question also seemed fairly uncalled-for, but it was intended as a compliment, an opening, an invitation. Had he travelled? or written something, perhaps . . .? Marina had an extraordinary gift for making everything she discussed sound insignificant. She dragged him into one shop after the next, where she bought nothing; then, when the hour came at which they all usually met at the café, she suggested they should give it a miss.

"Let's just be us, I like talking to you . . ."

Marco didn't doubt it, in fact it was she who did all the talking.

They ate alone in a small restaurant on the Giudecca. Then they walked a little, talking superficially and about nothing. In this way they passed a few strange and slightly insipid hours. Marco twice tried to enter her monologue, to share the intimacy offered him by Marina through her revelations; but the first attempt was foiled by a fresh recital of slanders, with the addition of episodes and details; the second died on his lips from sheer boredom.

With no enthusiasm on the part of either, they found themselves in bed together at Marina's house. It could be anybody here in my place, thought Marco, and she's probably thinking the same. But from the very first kisses he felt he was capable of holding her in his arms, and even believing in her. Caressing her, he thought: this is a beautiful woman. But the intimacy was still too fragmentary, too incoherent to trust; the crumbs of pleasure that had collected between the sheets prevented him from relaxing, he wanted to get up, shake out the covers, eliminate all traces.

Marina made love-talk, made promises, and described a host of lovely things for their future. Marco could not decide whether the eroticism and the talk were the product of pleasure or of slavish habit; he felt only bitterness of heart, because such fatuousness enabled Marina to take her pleasure, and to talk, while he couldn't even manage that. He had been too alone, and for too long; it was impossible for him not to distrust Marina's words – they seemed overblown – and this undesired attentiveness on the part of his intelligence seemed to him the biggest obstacle between them. "Bodies contain human beings, and their ideas," he told himself, so as not to ridicule Marina, who was talking about love. He forced himself to keep silent and to caress her – were he to talk he would become too serious for that bed; nothing would come of speaking but resentment, distrust, envy for the tranquil banality which, with all its lies, made Marina so self-possessed.

Distrust and resentment, however, did not prevent him from starting to see her regularly, albeit at an ever later hour in order to avoid talking and thinking as much as possible. Marina was there waiting for him, always with that stereotyped little smile of mockery mixed with rancour, a smirk which said, "When it comes down to it, my friend, you, with all your grey matter, are just a shit like all the rest." These meetings became a habit for both of them, a part of life, something to round off the day. Afterwards, sleep came, and the morning brought another day. Marco went home to his translating, Marina, who got a little money from her parents to keep her studying, filled in her time as best she could.

Their friends thought well of the match – they had doubtless tumbled to their relationship after that first evening when they'd not turned up at the usual hour. Something extremely primitive made them recognize Marco, now that they knew his sexual tastes, as one of the herd, one of them. All controversy ceased, and Marco thought that perhaps now they would all be on more familiar terms. But habit remained the only real reason for their gathering, as much for him as for them. Sitting at the café table sipping an aperitif, Marco tried to dilute his ideas with some commonplace, to hide his true opinions with a "Well I never!" about the life passing before his eyes, remote, packaged, futile as a television programme. When in the evenings he took part in those hours spent among many and nobody, he found himself constantly overcome by that same lazy, reticent vacuity which he had noticed in the others from the start, a strange kind of sleep that is never quite attainable. He was trying to edge back into conventionality, into fashionable opinions, to abdicate from his own world in favour of an illusory one which could do without him.

"It should be better than this," he burst out occasionally to Marina. "My life, yours, the world. How can we all let ourselves be dragged into this mediocrity?"

Marina would listen to him, more attentive to his passionate tone of voice than to the meaning of his words. Then it was her turn to grow lazy, and say to him with a sarcastic smirk, "Come here, and I'll console you."

Marco didn't want to be consoled. He wanted to understand and to be understood. He should never have begun that sort of discussion, shouldn't have spoken. He should have let the days, the true tillers of time, dismantle his dreams one by one, rob him of expectations and desires, until he desired no longer, no longer expected anyone. So, clumsily, Marco attempted to climb out of the dark and silence of his solitude into a day to be shared with his fellow men.

4

Luca and Nina made love wherever they could, as best they could, with no notion of what a clitoris was or whether or not the foreskin was more sensitive than the armpit; their kisses lasted for hours at a stretch and spoke of nothing but love love love, eyes tight shut. After that all-night absence there had been such violent scenes with their families that they were both now far too scared to think of another night together; they held afternoon trysts. Yet that night at Marco's (true, they'd hardly exchanged two words with him, yet they considered him an intimate friend), that night had taken on the aura of a fairy-tale; they often spoke of it and planned in some remote future to seek out that gentleman and go to live with him. Luca spoke of these fantasies so seductively that Nina just sat there listening happily, although the transformation set in motion by Marco's look and gesture had gone on growing and it was already possible to imagine a Nina stepping out alone in life, without parents or Luca, without anyone – a Nina rapidly evolving out of the adolescent fantasies which see reality as a construction outside a person, and to which one must eventually conform.

In her solitary games and her reading, which she had been passionately fond of since childhood, Nina had cultivated a secret world that was now visible in her eyes. Her father and her teachers had started to attack her, trying to force her to repress the character clearly legible in her gaze; it threatened them with its freshness, with the wealth of its observation of adult habits and preoccupations, made over the year during which she was excluded from the conventions of the adult world. Nina flew to Luca partly because he was the only male who showed her no hostility, and this from the beginning was for her more beautiful than their love.

Her father felt betrayed by her growing up, by the separation that would one day be the inevitable outcome of her maturity. He had married to find shelter from the mutability of things, and now the rapidity with which his daughter changed in thought and speech frightened him. Their arguments were usually petty and about things that neither of them understood. Nina found her mother was always on her side and later on her grandmother as well. It seemed there existed some code of behaviour which her father did not share, almost another culture which had a separate life and was never expressed for fear of being denied, but which came to the surface in times of conflict and was the basis for their alliance.

Nina had always been exceedingly bored by school, but she had quickly grasped what was expected of her and put it into practice, and had had no trouble getting good marks. It was only lately that studying had been made more difficult by the antagonism shown her by her teacher, Michele Scarpa, one of the Café Serafini's most assiduous habitués.

Dr Scarpa was not clear as to his tendencies and feared having to come to terms with a romantically dramatic homosexuality which would have put him on a par with the protagonists of his literary myths. He hid himself in this fear, neutralizing his desires with falterings and faint-heartedness. This, however, did not satisfy his impulse, which manifested itself instead in a questionable attitude both towards women

34

(whom he scorned, a sentiment frequently reciprocated), and towards the possible goals of his sexual reorientation, men to whom he neither spoke nor made any kind of advance, confining himself to an intense inquisitorial stare reminiscent of young Hamlet as portrayed in some never-to-be-forgotten performance by a second-rate actor.

Nina's thirst for affection, which was one of the most savage traits to be read in her eyes, attracted and frightened Scarpa, who perceived a solution to his own indecision in the force of her desire. But to admit that teacher and pupils were members of the same species – humankind – was utterly beyond Scarpa. After sweating blood to escape from the condition of being scolded, pulled up and chastised to that of meting out punishment and instruction? – not on your life!

A convenient outlet for his desires already existed in the classroom and he certainly didn't lack for ways of expressing the interest which Nina provoked in him. In just a few short weeks his predilection for Nina became a real obsession, and during oral tests he could no longer resist asking her, "So what were you up to last night, Contin, instead of studying? Out with some boy, I suppose." And then he'd invite her to put the same embargo on her love life as he had on his; "Get some work done, instead of gadding about," became the obsessive keynote of his scoldings and of his sexual repression.

Luca was in the same class as Nina, and was another of Scarpa's favourite victims, but for different reasons. Luca's father was a government lawyer and had been transferred the previous year to Venice from Rome, a city for which Scarpa at that time felt an intense loathing without really knowing why; then there was also the fact that Luca was studying music. In short, he possessed all those privileges which had inspired the teacher, during his youth, to dream of a new society which would chastise the decadent heirs of greatness (a condition which in Scarpa's opinion could only be inherited, being a thing of the past), and bestow on him what it took from others. Not only had there been no revolution but, frightened by the alliance which his imaginary socialism would have forced him to create with the truly disinherited – those for whom revolt is an immediate necessity, and Scarpa's role in it a problem of very secondary interest – he had retracted his most extremist views, and had entrenched himself in a cowardly, slightly hybrid reformist position, which was, after all, one of the features of his class.

But even if there hadn't been a revolution, there was nothing to prevent him personally punishing the handful of damned bourgeois who came within his range. In the literary vision of society which Scarpa had formed at university, the bourgeoisie was not defined by wealth or power, but by the image stemming from his own frustration. His chief enemies were writers, poets, musicians and film-directors, for all of whom he had a label, the triteness of which did not diminish its waspishness: "He's bourgeois." He would never have called an industrialist or a banker by such a name, indeed he would have been unable to find any word for them, so remote were they from his little world of make-believe. In his vocabulary the bourgeoisie had by now lost all historical meaning and simply become the force of evil, dwindling year by year into a uniform, indistinct negative, in which the various theories became so confused that they forced him to cling hysterically to platitudes as his gospel.

Luca, both because of his supposed privileges, and of an inborn antipathy to study, gave Scarpa a perfect opportunity to amuse himself in cruel homilies whenever he caught him with a subject poorly prepared. He reminded Luca of the abuses and the privileges of his class, and humiliated him with parodies of his stumbling answers. But there were deeper roots to Scarpa's dislike of Luca: they lay in the irresistible temptation to torture him. It isn't hard to wound a young person, but it takes a conscience to hold back from systematic persecution, and courage to break loose from the anger which is only a cover-up for the damage already done. Having but little of such resources to call upon, Scarpa became more and more enslaved by his vicious habit.

On the first day of school, which was also one of Luca's very first days in Venice, the boys and girls who already knew each other from the middle school had paired off at the desks, boys with boys in the two rows to the left of the teacher and girls in the third row. The only empty place left was beside Nina but Luca remained standing until the teacher, having entered the classroom and sat down at his desk, saw him still hovering and asked: "What are you doing still on your feet?"

"Where shall I sit, sir?"

"There, of course. Do you want to sit on the window-sill? Come along, come along now, she won't eat you," concluded the teacher, laughing as if such shyness were the oddest thing in the world; as if to show the class how exaggerated was this sort of bashfulness, to make fun of that odd-one out and win an unkind smile from his classmates, who were ready enough to laugh at the newcomer's predicament and quite prepared to back up their teacher's sarcasm.

Nina was writing Latin cribs in biro on the back of her hand. She wore a little woollen dress that came half-way down her thighs, and she had the strangest odour, which Luca later learnt was some cosmetic, but which for a long time he took to be a well-known brand of glue. What possible reason this girl could have for smearing herself with glue before coming to school seemed to him an enigma far more worthy of solution than those put forward by the teacher. It made her easily the most interesting human being in the class, so when one day during break, Luca found the little box of eye-shadow under the desk and sniffed at it, he felt he was smelling the commonplace, smelling mortality itself. All the theories he had formulated about the mysterious customs of his desk-mate crumbled at the discovery of this habit so common among young girls; he watched them disintegrate with that same disappointment and disillusionment with which one accepts the end of a dream and the silent re-emergence of the outlines of the bed. This odour increased day by day, and was now so intense that Luca felt he was living in a cloud. It was the scent of a grown-up woman who wears make-up . . . He should find a way to tell her this, because it would undoubtedly please her.

He felt incredibly lonely during that time; he missed his friends in Rome, his neighbourhood, and was filled with a strong, confused emotion which he could not put into words; and even if he could have, who was there he could tell, and why?

Once, when he had left his textbook at home, he had the chance to share Nina's, and to touch her arm, and press his leg against her thigh. The hour passed magically. He only hoped that Nina considered the touch accidental, or at least that she would not move away. "Why don't we embrace? Why not go to sleep in each other's arms?" he thought, and other sweet fantasies burgeoned from the fragrance of that make-up, while even the Greek grammar exercise seemed full of profound, decisive significance. When the hour was over, Luca gave thanks for it with a deep sigh, and swore never to bring his book again.

The effort of wrenching his thoughts away from the nostalgia for Rome and from the pleasing cloud of scents and sensations exuded by Nina made Scarpa's unspeakably tedious classes more difficult to follow day by day. Scarpa noticed this, and felt obliged to take the lad seriously in hand. He began to quiz him more often than the others, and to get him reading a passage aloud as soon as he saw him withdrawing into his melancholy. As he also wished to demonstrate the superiority of schools in northern Italy, he kept Luca's marks even lower than they would in any case have been. After scarcely a month Luca's situation at school was a catastrophe. First Scarpa, then the headmaster called in his parents. His absent-mindedness was becoming a problem about which he himself felt guilty, while his parents, the school, even a doctor, met to discuss the most strategic method of effecting a cure. But however much Luca tried to force himself to concentrate on Scarpa's lessons, which had an almost hypnotic effect on him, his eyes dropped in the end to Nina's legs, to her biro-scribbled hands, to the only human elements in that classroom which neither rejected nor punished him.

His reputation in class as a melancholy, absent-minded fellow, and above all an ignoramus, prevented him from making friends. His manners, habits, his very language, were all so very different from theirs that whenever he tried to start a conversation he either made them stand-offish or sent them into silly giggles as much as to say, "Brandi? He's nuts!"

As soon as Scarpa had thoroughly made up his mind about Luca, he told him to change desks. He put him at the back of the class with a boy about whom he never learnt more than his surname: Robazza. Separated from Nina's legs and hands, his gaze flew out of the window, to the grey skies, to the birdless trees in the courtyard. By slow degrees he began to feel himself truly lost in that classroom, and in that city. When questions were put to him he no longer managed to utter even the few things he did know; terrorized by the teacher, he could think of nothing but him. And the anguish of this fear did not abate when he went home, for his afternoons were spent in agonizing anticipation of the next morning.

With a perfect sense of timing, and fully conscious of his power, Scarpa stepped up the punishment. Implacable, unerring, his questions were now aimed at demonstrating Luca's weakness of character rather than testing his homework. The grilling turned from the matter of school marks to Luca's very personality – his laziness, absent-mindedness, glum disposition, his aloofness were described to the class so precisely by Scarpa that they seemed to the boy like the bars of a prison from which he would never escape again.

"And what will you do later on, if you don't learn something now?" his teacher asked him.

"True, what will I do?" Luca thought to himself, and found no answer. "Better to die now!"

He was informed that it was his friends in Rome who had been responsible for making him into such a hopeless case. And on the subject of Rome (the Black Hole of Italy, as Scarpa liked to call it), that city where no one works and each man is more wily than the last, the teacher vented his spleen, infused with a racialism and provincialism that he himself would have been the first to condemn in discussions at the Café Serafini.

Oppressed by fear, by all these proofs of his inferiority, and separated from Nina, Luca fled from school at the end of each morning. Even more painful than his low marks was having to make his way through the crowd of his classmates gathered outside the main gates, chattering happily about their loves and their plans for the afternoon from which he was excluded.

One day, towards the end of the geography hour, during which Scarpa had been blathering on in his usual incoherent, soporific fashion, Luca glanced at his watch. Only a few minutes to go till the end of the morning. He felt safe; he couldn't be interrogated at this point, and for once he would be able to go home without bearing bad news. He flicked through the pages of his geography text, vaguely looking at the pictures.

"Brandi," called Scarpa. "Come out here."

Luca looked around him incredulously, then, taking as long as he could over closing his books, he got up from his place and he went up to the master's desk. The bell rang, and for a second time he felt reprieved.

"Don't move!" Scarpa shouted angrily at the other pupils, who started putting away their books. "Tell me, Brandi, what are the principal economic resources of Colombia?"

The only thing Luca knew for certain about Colombia was that it was in South America; but he also knew that in order to give him any kind of mark the teacher would have had to ask at least two more questions, and he didn't have the time.

"I shall give you two out of ten, Brandi. You've been trying to bamboozle me. Do you think flicking through the book during the last five minutes of class is the way to prepare for questions?"

"I didn't think anything."

"That's enough. Don't make me say things in front of the class that I might regret. This way of behaving may have been all very well in Rome, but here we do things differently. The rest of you may go," he said, turning to the class. While his companions collected their coats in silence, so as to hear the dressing-down, Luca stood there trying in a weak voice to interrupt yet another account of his poor performance that term.

"It's time you understood, my dear Brandi, that here we do things differently. Take a look for yourself at the register. You haven't had a single pass-mark since the beginning of the school year. And don't say I haven't tried to help you,

41

and questioned you more often than the others, to give you the chance to catch up."

Luca looked at the register and nodded in acquiescence to the teacher's accusations. His classmates filed past one by one as they left the room, said goodbye to their teacher and glanced at Luca coldly, with the sham pity of those who cannot afford to speculate on the fate of one less fortunate than themselves. "Poor thing" they thought; but they could give themselves no time to feel solidarity with that "poor thing", because his misfortune was their good luck. Luca was acting as a lightning conductor for Scarpa's bad temper, and had it not been for that "poor thing" the ill temper would no doubt have fallen indiscriminately on them.

Nina was the last to leave, and before she had reached the door Scarpa made a point of saying in a loud voice, "And remember, you're here to listen to me, not to look at Nina Contin's legs."

So the bastard had noticed how often he looked at Nina's legs; he didn't have the delicacy to notice how beautiful her hands were, or the good smell emanating from her, but her legs he had indeed noticed. And that was why he had made him change places. Luca looked Scarpa in the eye; the tyranny of his professional mask was removed. The vulgar remark directed at Nina revealed a chink in his apparently impenetrable toughness, an inadequacy to which Luca felt superior. Beneath the black moustache he saw the lip trembling slightly, and could read frustration in every feature of that face; pathetic, hidden implications in every rebuke.

"I hope you don't imagine, sir, that your moustache can compare with Nina Contin's legs," he said, smiling serenely.

They stood like statues for a moment, except for Scarpa's now frantically trembling lip. Luca stared at it, on the verge of laughter. Scarpa raised an arm to strike him, but dropped it.

"Mind what you say, Brandi. Now get out," he muttered, covering his mouth with his hand. Luca gathered up his books and coat and left the classroom.

He was sorry about what would ensue from this episode, but remained impenitent. He was sorry that his mother would be sent for, and would have to suffer the humiliation of being told that her son was not only dumb and ignorant, but also impertinent. They would never tell her the truth, nor would she ever believe his version, for she could not possibly imagine that Luca's teacher was infatuated with a teenage girl, and was the boy's rival.

Nina was sitting on the Ponte delle Meravegie. As Luca approached her he made a wry face which was at once a greeting, an invitation, and an admission to being too tongue-tied to come out with it, so there was a touch of regret here too.

"Which way do you go to get home?" Nina asked.

"I live near the Frari."

"Good, we can go part of the way together. I live at the Tolentini."

Dumbstruck, Luca stood like a ninny, two paces behind Nina who had already set off towards San Barnaba. The fact is, he was convinced, along with Scarpa and his parents, that, alas, he was no more than a two out of ten in geography and the same in Greek, besides being a deadbeat and idler, and a Roman to boot. Nina, on the other hand, was the tops right across the board, she had it all, whether it was natural or acquired. He was so surprised that she had offered to keep him company part of the way home that he couldn't think of anything to say, and he found it hard to walk in a natural, co-ordinated way. They strolled side by side in silence, Luca sifting through his stock of worldly knowledge (which didn't add up to a row of beans) as he looked for a suitable topic of conversation, but everything he came up

43

with seemed childish and futile. So instead he gazed about him at the houses, the trees, the clouds, and said nothing. Every so often a word managed to surface from his thoughts and reach his lips, and he turned towards her. But by then the word wanted to be a kiss, and but for lack of courage it turned instead into a wide, amiable grin. This Nina loved straight off, for in it she read all the affectionate things he couldn't put into words.

"Scarpa treats you like a beast, doesn't he? He's really got it in for you."

But Luca didn't want to talk about school, didn't want to go over the latest incident and he could give no voice to his heart; all he could do was gaze at her.

Nina laughed, delighting in Luca's enraptured gaze. He thought of the fountains of St Peter's laughing in summer, when the rays of the sun turn the highest jets to azure, and his eyes followed the flow of her long, soft hair, which streamed from cheek to shoulder and down to her breasts, like that water pouring from one bowl to the next.

"Let's have a snack."

As she entered the *pasticceria*, Nina passed so close to him that the smell of her flesh and her make-up flooded over him a second time, and once again his mind dissolved in that haze of perfume. "Was she talking to me?" he thought, and as he looked at her the whole notion of reality, of the things one says and does, melted away, and was lost in the gentle vagueness of his desire – a desire still so pure and ignorant of itself that he allowed it to lead him through the streets in pursuit of a perfume.

Slowly, slowly, to the musical accompaniment of a city's lunch-hour preparations – tables being laid in houses and restaurants, shops shutting for the midday break – and to the sound of their feet beating questions and answers on the steps of the bridges, as they watched an empty fruit-box riding on the water, a playful sunbeam running up the walls, their mutual understanding wordlessly took on a subtle form; it was nameless as yet, unspoken, but both of them recognized it as it drew nearer to their hearts. An understanding existed, born of isolated gestures, of the certain knowledge of where the other's body was, and this, as they gazed at each other, created a more tangible reality where thoughts, fears, kindnesses, took shape in their expressions, so that a certain smile of Nina's could evoke the response: "She's happy," or "What on earth is she expecting?" or "Maybe she hasn't understood." All those feelings which Luca had tried to smuggle out through the window during Scarpa's classes and which for so long had found refuge in Nina's legs and hands – his yearning, his nostalgia for Rome, for places he had loved and had had to leave – these feelings at last found a resting place and a new freedom from fear in this new understanding, in the peace of Nina's eyes.

Luca took Nina home, then she walked back with him to his house, and at length they said "Goodbye, see you tomorrow," and parted. But all that afternoon and all that night they each thought of nothing but where the other was, and wondered about that other life which they could lay claim to and yet never possess. That other life moved parallel in time and yet invisible, remote, with other parents, other rooms, other thoughts. And while that other life taking place far away was being peopled by the imagination with fantasies, desires, and fears, this life before their eyes, so down-to-earth it was positively dull, seemed to lose content, consistency and significance, and the brief separation of an afternoon stretched into an unending, intolerable torture. But tomorrow would be beautiful, the sun would sound the trumpets of the morning for them, and even school would become a place of marvels, for there was Nina, and there was Luca; and there too was poor Scarpa, bawling at ghosts, at the wooden legs of non-existent women.

The days flowed one into the next. Time, in which we feverishly search for an hour's peace, a moment's safety, began to course along like a rapid stream, offering glimpses of a summer in which there would be no obstacle in the way of those walks, of seeing each other home, nothing to hinder that mutual trust in which their lives had truly begun.

Scarpa took no action after the incident with Luca, and for several weeks scarcely seemed to know how to behave, ignoring his presence in class. Luca, heartened by his friendship with Nina, faced his oral tests and homework with greater confidence, and managed to slip through the tight net of Scarpa's rancour, winning a grudging admission of improvement. Scarpa naturally took all the credit for this, and went back to venting his tyranny indiscriminately on the anonymous rabble.

Luca's parents felt responsible, first towards their son who had so obviously suffered from the move, and secondly towards society, which would have little use for a Luca as scatter-brained and lazy as he; but they felt relieved of both responsibilities when his results showed some improvement, and they were glad to re-establish the respectable, formal, unemotional dealings with their son to which they were all accustomed.

Avvocato Brandi had made a hobby of the study of medieval history, and his relationships with the world were all interpreted in terms of the canons and conventions by which he deemed that epoch to have been ruled. His wife shared his habit and, being totally clueless about Communists, Social Democrats and reactionaries, she constantly attempted to translate any political discussion into the grammar of the world she knew, where power was divided between Guelphs and Ghibellines as between conservatives and progressives.

Luca's sister Silvia was four years younger than himself and, like him, studied the piano; since she scarcely ever opened her mouth, it was possible to credit her with every virtue which, less out of innate modesty than out of the habit of silence, she neither flaunted nor denied.

Nina gave her father as little chance as possible of getting at her; she instinctively tried to keep out of his way and avoid conversation, because she felt she wounded him with every word, even with the deepening timbre of her voice as she grew and matured. She slid from bed to school every morning, trying to avoid him about the house. She was on her feet and clearing the table the instant she had swallowed a few hasty mouthfuls, like a little fish darting out of the fisherman's grasp. Only Luca's telephone calls still gave her father a chance to grumble, for Luca telephoned every evening, and shielded by distance, his talk was an endless freewheeling fantasy. Nina knew the tone of voice her father would use if they got into an argument; she could feel he was jealous, and didn't want to give him a chance to explode. So the moment he started to ask how much longer she would be on the phone, she hastily said goodbye to Luca and shut herself in her room. She understood her father very little, could not imagine what his life was like, and felt he had no friends, no love for anything, and was just as bear-like and quarrelsome with everything and everybody. Yet she did not doubt that he was a kind-hearted man.

That winter there was a good deal of talk about an Italian film, set in Paris, with a great American actor in the leading role. These facts alone were enough to persuade Scarpa that it must be a masterpiece. The courts had threatened to burn all existing copies for obscenity – such persecution was an added spice for the numerous under-age cinema-goers who defied public opinion and sought damnation at the movies.

Nina and Luca decided that they too would try to see the film. Nina looked a few years older than her age, but it was hard for Luca to pretend to be over eighteen. As it was carnival time, however, he turned up at the box-office in a false moustache, spectacles and a hat, which if anything made his age even more apparent. However, the woman in the box-office didn't insist on seeing any documents, and let them through. Once in the cinema, Luca paid very little attention to what was happening on the screen; only the scenes in which the American actor insulted the heroine, and the ones where they made love, held his interest. But immediately his thoughts turned to Nina and what she was thinking about the film; whether she felt she was faced with an irresistible masterpiece, or with a series of disgusting scenes which she would hold against him for ever after. On leaving the cinema, to his great relief, Nina said the film was beautiful, partly because she hadn't understood a single thing the actors had said to each other, and partly because it was always easier to agree with Scarpa who had praised the movie in class with words of many syllables; but especially because Luca's disguise had done its job, and made her feel that they actually were eighteen.

So as not to break the thread of discoveries stemming from their new-found age, they went into an *osteria* and ordered a bottle of red wine. By now Luca was laughing gaily and telling her nonchalantly about those fantasies that until then he had only managed to impart to her over the telephone. Nina laughed too; she knew how fragile their love was and that it subsisted only on the fragments of time saved from school and family, moments that eluded the repression of the adult world, but this did not worry her unduly. The things they said to one another would perhaps never become reality, but they gave her a glimpse of a world which was so vastly preferable to the one being thrust upon her that this laughter with Luca was worthwhile if only as a way of seeing another side to Scarpa and to her father. Luca's false moustache fell into his glass as he laughed, and Nina fished it out and stuck it on her own lip.

"Now, Brandi, tell me the principal economic resources of Colombia." For a second Luca sensed the fear and loneliness of his first months in that city returning to catch in his throat like vomit. "This wine makes me sick, and so does Nina," he thought; but the next instant Nina looked beautiful to him, and funny with her moustache, and the wine settled agreeably in his belly.

"Fancy being pretty even in a moustache!"

"Why *even*? Don't you find Scarpa handsome?" asked Nina, twitching her upper lip like the teacher. She little realized that this joke was breaking the thread that bound Luca to her, that thoughts could no longer surface naturally as they talked, but slid back into a tangle of inhibitions, so that now Luca would rather have been speaking to her on the telephone than face to face. He realized in that moment that they could not always be on the same wavelength, that Nina could hurt him and still laugh and the idea struck him like a rap on the knuckles, like an absurd punishment inflicted by the person he trusted. Magnified and distorted by the wine, this notion tormented him. He felt that in echoing the general opinion of the girls at school about Scarpa's austere good looks, Nina was moving away from him, disappearing back into that silly world of gossip in the corridors which he loathed. Another instant, and the thoughts which prevented him meeting Nina's eyes dispersed, as when in March a cloud passes for a moment across the sun, and Nina once again seemed crystal clear, generous, incapable of wounding him. Maybe he himself had created a non-existent barrier; his own mental short-circuit had severed their understanding, not Nina. Maybe it was the wine that severed the coherence and the continuity, and divided time into intense fragments, falling out of sequence. He gulped down another mouthful, trying to make the alcohol focus his imagination on the highest beauty and love, feeling his heart, his stomach, his bowels lurch like ships with madmen at the helm, prone to the most incredible manoeuvres amid storms and to unaccountable shipwrecks in calm seas.

By the time they set off for home, it was well past supper time. Campo San Bartolomeo was crowded with people in carnival costumes, passing great bottles of wine from hand to hand. Luca lost Nina and started looking for her, swigging down huge gulps of wine every so often to steady his stomach. Half an hour passed, perhaps more, while Luca staved off a sense of desertion by lapsing into a daze. "It's a party, she's having fun," he thought, and drifted in the moving currents of people from one side of the square to the other, trying to keep from thinking, because the first thought that came into his head was that Nina had gone off and left him. Some antic in the crowd would distract him for a minute, then he'd resume his search. He thought maybe he had caught sight of her waving, but the crowd was too dense, he couldn't reach her, and was swept in another direction. He turned round, and Nina was right behind him.

"Don't disappear like that, Luca!" Nina grabbed his hand, and in that grasp he felt secure. The crowd dissolved as in a dream, and once again there was only the night, and silence. A gentle wind blew over the city, carrying away with it the hours, the fears, the dust which settles on the heart in the long moments of melancholy. A kindly, playful wind, whispering incomprehensible, seductive words into their ears, blew shyness away and freed them from their customary politeness. Behind Santa Margherita, Luca, already tall as a young sapling, bent down to Nina's lips and spoke the word that had been lost in his smiles. And then the stars were no longer in the sky, but were there behind his closed eyes and in the taste of flower dew which Nina's kisses distilled upon his mouth. And Luca was the sky itself, boundless and empty, each element shattering into a thousand fragments, spreading out to encompass everything, and was falling, falling, falling towards the only rose in that tiny planet. He leant over so far that he fell to the ground. And, as when a dream stops short, abandoning us in our beds, we are eager to escape into the day and take refuge in things of little matter, so Luca, seeing that the stars were not after all in his closed eyes, nor in the lips which were now poised over him, laughing, but up there, distant and cold, now felt he had to flee, to catch at least a fragment of that shattered sky.

He ran and hid behind the first corner. Who knows how many people had seen that kiss, or how they had laughed at it? Certainly they would have guessed it was his first. But had he really done it? Had he really kissed Nina, or only imagined it — a shadow lost among the street-lamps, a night-time fancy escaping from the open windows of other lovers? The city was silent and deserted, and the only sound was of Nina's light footsteps as she chased after him.

"What's wrong? Where are you running off to?" They burst out laughing, propping each other up like two thieves after a raid, their breath mingling. The running, the excitement and the wine made Luca's stomach heave with increasing violence, and he began to feel cold and to vomit; he had turned very pale and was drawling a confused muddle of words. Nina thought the best thing was to get him home; she leant him up against the door of his house, rang the bell and made off. Luca crouched on the step and watched her go.

It was eleven forty-five; his mother had been worrying since eight o'clock. She had tried without success to discover his whereabouts by telephoning first Nina's parents, then the hospitals and eventually the police. Luca's father had dealt with this last call, although to tell the truth he wasn't unduly worried. He had resolved anyway to punish his son for causing his mother so much anxiety. But when they found him there drunk, babbling incoherently the names of Scarpa, the American actor and Nina, they put him to bed without saying a word.

At dawn Luca lay listening to the confused chorus of the birds, watching the clear light seep through the shutters; he wasn't aware of having awoken. His legs, his arms, his stomach and chest hurt him, and his senses were still deadened by the wine, but his mind was clear. He watched that first light outline, the shape of his discarded clothing on the chair, slice the closed air of the room into so many stripes of shadow and slivers of light. He got up, opened the window and took in a deep breath. The sun rose and Luca lay down in the rumpled bed to enjoy its warmth on his face, the day-warmth, it seemed, of a fairy-tale genie bending over his cheek to caress it. He fell asleep again, and when he woke the day was different; his good genie had given place to the sound of coffee cups from the kitchen summoning Silvia and himself to breakfast. It was freezing – he'd have to get up and shut the window and, worse still, face his parents.

"Have you gone mad?" shouted his mother, coming into the bedroom and stepping straight across to close the window. "You an eskimo or something? Do you want to catch pneumonia? Quick, get dressed, or you'll be late for school." From under the bedclothes Luca eyed her precise, rapid movements, and listened to the shrill tone her voice acquired when she wanted him to do something in a hurry.

"You went off the rails last night, eh? Your father was so worried he even rang the police. Run and apologize before he goes out, otherwise he'll be in a bad mood all day." She picked his shirt off the floor while she was speaking and looked at the collar with mild disgust. Then she sat down on the edge of the bed, searching his eyes to find out how deeply he was entrenched beneath the bedclothes that morning. She ran her fingers through his hair. Luca loathed this gesture. When she caressed him like that it was impossible to feign illness or exhaustion; its tenderness unmanned him and took the edge off any excuse he could have raked up for not going to school. So that in the end, it became the only reason for his getting up and agreeing to return to the beastly place.

He got out of bed, pulled on his shirt, his trousers, his shoes, and felt that already he was a stranger to himself; as this same stranger he went and mumbled penitent words to his father. He washed the stranger's face, and cleaned its teeth, gave it its morning coffee and reluctantly followed it in the race to reach school before the porter shut everybody in, prisoners for five long hours at the mercy of their teachers. About this other self all he thought was "They certainly make you run." Nina was not there, so the morning passed slowly and insipidly, the classroom once again that hostile foreign country of his first months in Venice.

Unluckily for Nina she had not been drunk enough to collapse on the floor when she got home, but sufficiently so for her father to lay into her with all the pent-up fury accumulated during those past months of non-communication.

"You filthy whore, you, where've you been out this late? Look at those black lips, you slut. Tell me where you've been with your fancy man, eh? Answer me, you piece of filth! Do you want to kill me? Take that!" He slapped her again and again, and was yelling so loud that even if Nina had said anything, no one would have heard her. She covered her face with her hands and wept; she tried to find the courage to get out from under the blows, but something held her there, the fear of bringing home to her father the impotence expressed in his hands, and of humiliating him. "What will become of me in this world if even you treat me like this?" she thought to herself, but said nothing. Her mother stood stock-still, watching that scene; she was far more frightened even than Nina by the violent change that had come over her husband in the last months and dared not interrupt his outburst. But the awareness of his own impotence and of the contradiction between his blows and his feelings, of how little the one had to do with the other and especially with Nina – this awareness became almost instantly hard and brittle, like plaster drying. Pietro remained motionless for some seconds, prisoner of a mask; he knew he had got some things wrong with Nina, perhaps everything, and he felt ashamed, and also ashamed of his remorse.

"Go to bed, damn you!" he shouted at Nina, and when she didn't move, he beat his head against the wall and began to cry while Maria, Nina's mother, instinctively mouthed a soundless incantation, "Mother of God, don't let him go mad, I beg you, don't let my husband go mad." She followed the words with her mouth and heart, less to invoke any god, but rather to exorcize the monstrous void which her husband's madness would leave. The age-old phantom of poverty, which she had always felt hovering over their heads because of their complete lack of resources beyond those of her husband's salary as a clerk, seemed to her now, in the wake of Pietro's furious blows and ensuing tears, to hold a certain menace. It was there in the white wall against which Pietro had turned his head to weep. Unable to free himself of the pain in any other way, he looked to that wall for solace. But walls cannot bring solace, Maria knew that; they are cold and Nina too watched her father's shoulders shaking with sobs, and like her mother felt unable to touch him. Those shoulders were hunched now in a long curve, as if the neck were no longer able to support the weight of the head and the arms, and wanted only to let them sag slowly to the floor. "How old he's getting," she said to herself, and laid a hand on his back.

"Go away, you devils, both of you, and leave me in peace," yelled Pietro, opening the door and flinging himself downstairs. Later that night Nina heard him come back in, heard him talk and weep again with her mother, and from her bed, from the stillness that had entered into her thoughts, she wished him a little peace and sleep.

In the morning she got up and dressed hurriedly, left the house with her books under her arm, and raced to school. But the big doors were already closed when she arrived, so she set off at a slow pace towards the Frari, retracing the beautiful walks she and Luca had discovered together. But now the lapping water, the noises from the houses (those bottled up hell-holes) all seemed sad sounds; and the remorse she felt at not having been able to speak to her father set her mouth in an ugly line which wouldn't go away. Last night's wine had turned to acid in her stomach and in her thoughts. As she reviewed the evening with Luca, it seemed to her she could lay the blame for what had happened on that stupid idea of going to see a forbidden film; and then the wine and that wretched carnival that had wasted so much time. But when she remembered their first kiss she lost all sense of guilt, and as she ran through the events, it seemed that it had all been bound to happen and nobody was to blame for anything.

55

That cold morning dragged on endlessly – shop-windows, empty hours, hurrying people. When at last it was one o'clock, she went to meet Luca, who invited her to lunch with his parents.

"Ah, so you are Nina," Signora Brandi said, showing her where to hang her coat in the hall. "We're just waiting for my husband, then we can sit down. Do you want to ring home to tell your parents you are having lunch with us?"

"No, thank you, my parents let me do what I like."

"Even get into the kind of state Luca was in last night?"

"Oh, that doesn't happen to me; I can hold my wine all right."

Nina felt torn in two by every question Luca's mother asked: one half of her wanted to be friendly, to smile and chat in a way she was not used to, with the kind of charm which for her was an abstract idea, something she had only read about. The other half was burdened with thoughts of her father and the scene he would make this time, after her failure to turn up for lunch. And although the sociable half was completely artificial and forced smiles and facial expressions quite external to her – stemming from the demands of the conversation rather than from her true feelings – she was unable to stop being this puppet, or to free herself from its insufferable falsity, so that in the end she was completely at the mercy of that invisible puppeteer holding the strings, and felt a desperate urge to weep and scream, to let them know who she really was. But the puppeteer had no intention of letting her change her role, and Nina was paralysed by a vague sense of shame about her social standing, as if she had hidden her family away in the back of the shop while she served this important client.

All that emerged from Nina's dilemma was a slight air of affectation, and because of this, Luca's parents didn't much take to her; she seemed to them bogus. Nina could feel this antipathy all through the meal and tried to compensate by exaggerating those phony, refined gestures which, according to strange notions she had at that age gained about the world, constituted good manners.

After lunch was over Nina cried a little with Luca in his room, without speaking and perhaps for no reason. They lay down together in the little bed where, with kiss upon kiss, embrace upon embrace, they would bare themselves to each other day after day, and come to know each other. But for that afternoon they did no more than repeat that long, fresh kiss which had bloomed on the lips of Nina and caused Luca to fall out of the sky.

The evolution that they both sought so urgently remained sealed in that room. Held back by school, and by relations with their parents (which seemed destined to get worse), Nina and Luca could only grow in their hearts and through their words, in a world which offered them no scope to prove themselves. They would grow to a point where they could no longer tolerate life keeping them apart, crushing them with schoolwork which seemed to have the sole purpose of making them similar to their elders and preventing them from taking their own view. It was only by accident that they were allowed to live, in those few hours no one checked up on them: afternoons of study, solitary nights in which they kept watch over the future, trying to guess the shape of the thing they could not yet see.

5

Now that Marco had made up his mind to try to live once more among people and things, during the daylight hours, when social life is the measure of time, his obsessions had subsided of their own accord. His visions, dreams and worries were held at bay by everyday commitments, and the life of that other world, which had absorbed him for so long, touched him only sporadically. Only a fragment of speech, an instant at sunset, or a detail in someone's face occasionally crossed the threshold, like a prisoner jumping the fence, and brought him back among the roots of his sensibility.

He didn't pay much heed to these brief interludes, pre-occupied as he was by the effort to identify the reality he held in common with other men. The daily paper, the company in the Café Serafini and Marina had therefore become the means of studying the society he wished to partake of again. But as with all projects of this nature, which were embarked upon as the gratuitous exercise of a method rather than from a genuine desire to achieve a given object, it was once again not the world outside himself which grew clearer, but his own penchant towards solitude. Ideologies and religions seemed incomprehensibly tangled in the opinions of the world around him; the one thing clear to him was the similarity of the methods expounded by the adherents of one creed or the other. By comparison, his own flights of fancy had far more consistency, but Marco tried not to make such comparisons, and of his months spent wandering by night there remained only a vague, confused memory of sorrow, of death looming and inevitable. Moreover he was afraid that if he let himself relapse into the contemplation of emptiness, he would never escape again, he would remain a prisoner of the night, of the unspoken thought. From eating to defecating, from talking to sleeping and making love, everything was now instant activity, chopped into bits and carried away in the rush. As he gradually returned to the life of an ordinary person who works, eats, makes love, sleeps at the proper times, his existence was reduced to physiological acts, to the satisfaction of his bodily needs. Where they came from, what they were made of and how they arose was of no great consequence, he simply dealt with the pleasure and pain as if they were unwanted growths, avoiding the confrontation of a searching, prying intellect that dug, imagined, invented.

It was in his relationship with Marina that this want of substance was most painfully evident: in those loveless embraces during which a tender word was never uttered (and if it had been, they would probably have hurried away from each other in embarrassment), and in the consummation of a pleasure that was daily carrying them further and further apart. Apathy and inertia kept them together until they were smothered by silence and the weight of things unsaid. The weaker their union became, the more Marina praised its delights and qualities, as if overcome by panic and the premonition of an end lacking any drama save that of being undramatic. After making love they turned away, each to his own side of the bed, waiting for sleep and dreaming of some other lover, as if with someone else those same deficiencies might appear in a better light. By this time nothing filtered through the rancour that lay festering in each of them but a series of feeble compliments: What a man! You delicious woman! And weariness advanced upon them.

But in the world where Marco was trying to hew himself out a place, there was nothing to gainsay such wretchedness, so that in returning to her he felt he was returning to the inevitable, to what any other woman would have given him, as if women were not people endowed with separate personalities, but merely a species with which his own, the male, had relationships according to fixed rules.

An occasional relic of beauty appeared in his day, like treasure washed ashore from some wreck: the echo of the sun's cry as it drowned in the sea, the whispered conversation of two old men, the pungent smell of the lagoon, would sometimes penetrate the guard he kept over his senses and move him for an instant, by chance. Then he would remember that once he had felt more joy in reading, or listening, had had more heart to join in life. Nowadays he tired of things at once, frustrated by the brevity of such moments, incapable of following the evolution and the resolution of situations, and frantically switching his attention from one thing to another in search of the climax of an emotion which instead became ever weaker and in the end died altogether.

In his musings upon music or literature he began to recognize certain Scarpa-esque expressions; the mannerisms, the generalizations that lost the point of the argument, the insignificant details that filled the mouth like an excess of saliva. Scarpa-fashion, he found himself insisting on the analysis of such and such a passage, or on "those two lines on page nine hundred and thirty-three", which contained meanings no better and no different from those expressed by the author two lines before or after. But rather than be relegated to solitude, Marco decided to ignore how he had acquired such rhetoric, smothering his disdain for his own destiny with an "Oh well, anyway . . ." picked up from Marina.

An article of his on a film directed by a cherished hero of the group caused a long discussion in the Café Serafini.

"Marco Ivancich is so little in love with life that he can't even recognize when someone makes a good film these days," said Scarpa, his voice carrying the weight of his understanding of the work. "The best ideas of our generation are condensed in this film: our radicalism, our desire to penetrate beyond the traditional contrasts of western culture with the stylistic elegance of one who truly understands this culture from the inside, and at all levels."

Marina was the first to nod her head and thought how fortunate were the students of this leading light, to learn about western culture from the inside.

"It certainly is a very beautiful film, at every level," interjected Bortoletti from time to time, in an earnest attempt to enliven the conversation. Beniamino Bortoletti, a recent graduate in the History of Cinema, had secured himself a regular column in the local paper; his weekly article expressed his unconditional enthusiasm for each and every film, and at all levels. Bortoletti had held Scarpa in the highest esteem ever since the time when, during their first years at university, they had met in a public debate in the Great Hall of the School of Architecture. This highly animated but inconclusive debate was on the theme of "Art and the Masses". Amid the complete indifference of the participants and the total anarchy of the speakers, Scarpa and Bortoletti had hurled first unintelligible and then merely obscure opinions at one another. When they discovered what they were talking about, they found themselves in immediate agreement. The opinion, if opinion it be, was that art was bourgeois, the masses were not, therefore art would be destroyed by the Revolution. Their supposed audience had left the hall halfway through the discussion, well before the two orators had defined the concepts of Art and the Masses sufficiently to find a place in the welter of words they were pouring on each other's heads. When Scarpa at last became aware that Bortoletti was the only person listening to his thesis, and fearing that a new objection might delay the lunch-break even further, he crept forward and without interrupting his speech took Bortoletti by the arm. In a warmer and less formal tone he concluded: "Not everyone has the preparation to engage in a discussion on such an important and delicate subject." Bortoletti responded with a happy wink, and in the secret depths of his soul he swore loyalty to the man who had first recognized his talents. Since then, whenever he had a thought which departed from Scarpa's ideas, he examined his conscience to discover the point at which he had gone astray.

When Marco joined the learned gathering he provoked a sudden silence; Marina was hanging on Scarpa's every word; her attention was so riveted that she failed to notice Marco's greeting. Excited by that stare, the teacher immediately determined to give her a demonstration of his intellectual prowess.

"My dear Ivancich, your latest article didn't please us one bit, did it, Bortoletti?"

"No way, at no level," assented his colleague.

"What didn't you like about it?" Marco asked.

Marina darted a cross glance at him, then fixed her gaze once more on to Scarpa's legs.

"You can't take us in like that, you know," the teacher continued relentlessly. "It's not a case of liking it or not, ideas are of no importance, we are concerned plainly and simply with recognizing certain facts. The Social Phenomenon can't be explained in words, as Bortoletti was saying before you arrived." Bortoletti, who had never in his life conceived such a long sentence, hastily tried to string together a little speech in order to enlarge on the opinion attributed to him. "One either acknowledges the Social Phenomenon," continued Scarpa, "or one does not."

"The Social Phenomenon cannot be explained in words," Bortoletti burst out, and then fell back in line with Scarpa's gaze, thus demonstrating his total solidarity, regardless of the question at issue.

"You know nothing about the Social Phenomenon, Ivancich. Your cosmopolitan experiences would be useless to you in the face of society. So just shut up."

"Why should I shut up? In my article . . ."

"Your article," Scarpa interrupted again, banging his fists on the table, then not quite knowing what to say after such a peremptory gesture. "Who gives a shit any more about your article! I repeat, this has nothing to do with words, it has to do with facts, with the experience of the Social Phenomenon."

"The Social Phenomenon cannot be explained in words," Bortoletti repeated automatically on hearing the word "phenomenon".

"I simply can't imagine why you're so worked up about this article," Marco said calmly.

"Oh Christ, you and your article! Can't you see, this is just another example of your bourgeois narcissism, as Marina so rightly said. When it comes down to it, Marco Ivancich, which side are you on?"

"Marina, d'you really know what narcissism means?" Marco asked in surprise.

"Stick to the point. Which side are you on?" said Marina, with a smirk that left no doubt as to which side she was on.

"But on which side of what?" Marco asked Scarpa.

"What do you mean, of what . . ." stammered the teacher, completely at sea. "Of daily life which changes . . ."

"My dear Scarpa, I have not the slightest wish to take sides for or against your daily life, which incidentally doesn't seem to have changed noticeably at any stage."

Scarpa longed for the day when he would be able to take this bourgeois to court, and he cast rapid glances at Marina to assure himself of her loyalty to the cause. Marina was in any case well trained in the art of acting out petty comedies, and had already forgotten that she had been sleeping with Marco up until the night before, promising him fidelity and a future in the midst of her other prattle. Her betrayal was rapid, firm and unequivocal. Scarpa got up and left the bar, followed immediately by his entourage. Marina stared into Marco's eyes for a moment, shook her head significantly, then got up and joined the others.

That trite, cinematographic gesture made Marco laugh. But the moment she had left the bar he felt a tide of bitterness rising in him. Her skin, her lips, her breasts. "I don't love her, though," he thought, and the wretched memory of those tedious bouts of love-making he had undergone with her, those battles between body and mind in the interminable "I love her, I love her not" gave a ridiculous twist to everything, as if a clown had come on stage in his head to announce that this was no drama but merely a farce. The thought of Scarpa and Marina together made him smile. What a couple! She so ravenous, he so frigid, they wouldn't last together long enough to say goodnight.

Then a dumb, icy, colourless feeling invaded his spirits. He thought of the coming night and the solitude waiting for him like an undertaker. Impossible to get up from his chair, to leave that public place where people talked loudly, and for his benefit too, since they distracted him from his monologue of misery. He ordered a bottle of wine and began to drink it by himself, trying to glimpse, in the rupture that this sudden desertion had inflicted on the order of things, the way towards the guileless world of his own heart.

Reality had split in two, events rushing in one direction, his emotions in the other – Marina pursuing Scarpa, his own thoughts pursuing certain tragi-comic details that seemed to drip down the invisible wall which separated him from the world of the powerful and the rebellious, where together with his peers he struggled for a morsel of bread and a crumb of individuality. A detail of Marina's body, a shoulder, an ear, a buttock, or Scarpa's moustachioed lip, or some phrase that he had thought innocent or stupid, now slotted into place and suddenly wounded him. In details such as these the illusion that had kept those weeks together was shattered, the illusion that had allowed him to frequent that small, verbose company, to speak and live as they did. The judgments he had suspended in order to camouflage himself inside the group suddenly became clear: Scarpa was an authoritarian megalomaniac, Bortoletti his henchman, and all the others so much a part of the furniture that they had probably never worried about distancing themselves from it. But Marina, she was really somebody quite unique. All that stuff about physical love, those sentimental platitudes she had smothered him with after making love, and then that "Oh well, anyway!" and that "Oh come on!" and that "But so what?" with which she had shut him up whenever he tried to get a word in edgeways, were nothing but rituals of the group. She had tried to fit him into the company, this was what her love amounted to, but when she found she could not integrate him with Scarpa's provincial delirium, she abandoned him. Who was it then that had smiled at his kisses? Was it Marina who succumbed to pleasure, or was it a group hanger-on? Why cry over her then? Why break your heart over trifles? Yes, why –? And one by one the good reasons left him, like those intentions he had not long ago imagined rising from his bed and crashing against the wall like flies.

He drank slowly. Anger, sadness, the absurdity of it all became infused with the wine, until Marina, the others, the outward circumstances, all became part of the same mood, shapes in his roving thoughts; as when mist drifts over the plain, and merges buildings, trees, the earth, the cold in a single sensation that is no longer external and climatic but is gradually subsumed into one's spirit. During those weeks convention had buried his feelings deep in his heart, leaving mere traces and echoes. Now lucidity and all the other things he had put under lock and key as inappropriate to a worldlier regime came back to him like old friends who stay on to chat when the party is over. At last, Marco thought to himself, I shall be able to watch the sun set without feeling tired.

Two young people were standing by the table.

"Don't you recognize us?" the girl asked, laughing. Partly because of the wine, partly because he had no memory for faces, and mostly because of that laughter, which they had sent ringing through the alleys of the city, without him, for it had nothing to do with him, Marco failed to recognize them or to show the least sign of friendliness. He regarded them with a suspicious scowl, as if they were two policemen sent from the world outside, which he and his bottle were now forsaking. Then, owing to one of those lightning changes of mood that alcohol produces in one's perceptions, he saw them as two angels sent from heaven to open the gates of the world, the very gates in which he had just pinched his fingers. But he still didn't recognize them; he searched through his store of memories for that tone of voice, the luminous glance of the girl, the absent-minded expression in her friend, but unavailingly.

"We met one night last year," Nina said. Then Luca remembered too.

"Oh yes. You're Marco."

"True, I am Marco," Marco thought to himself, as if he had just discovered himself in Luca's irrefutable statement, and despite the fact that he still couldn't for the life of him think who they were, he invited them to join him.

"I'll order another bottle of wine, this is finished," said Luca, going off to the bar while Nina sat down next to Marco.

"How are things going?" she asked him quickly.

"Oh well, you know . . ." Marco answered, not wanting to think about it. But how his words dragged, what an effort it was to get them to his lips! The mixture of wine and bad temper made them stick in his throat; they came out slow and hoarse, and this annoyed him. Whereas Nina's words seemed to hop about on her tongue like sparrows on a lawn, light, fresh and simple. Too much effort, he thought, to meet this girl's gaze, to bring himself back from the expanses in which he had been blindly groping to the person before him, to this little woman addressing him with such familiarity. Who is she? And anyway, what does it matter?

"I'm here, Marco. Don't talk to yourself. Tell the truth, you really don't remember, do you?"

"Here, have some of this," Luca interrupted, filling her glass.

"Luca, he doesn't remember us," sighed Nina, disappointed. "Just wait, you'll remember. I'll tell you all about it." Nina laughed again, for no reason. Her laughter seemed kind to Marco now; by laughing at everything Luca said, Nina showed him her love. Marco saw that they were happy, that they understood each other on the instant, and

67

wanted to draw him into their intimacy. But as he noticed their love, which did not rebuff him but tried on the contrary to involve him, he realized that his heart had taken a step backwards.

"We were outside Nina's house."

"At the Tolentini," interrupted Nina.

"And we were kissing. Nina wanted me to go upstairs with her and kiss some more, because her parents were asleep and would never know. But I'm not that mad, I can tell you. If you saw Nina's dad you'd get my point."

"So, we come round the corner, and see you sitting on the steps, and you," Nina went on, "you don't budge, you won't let us pass."

"'I happened by chance to hear what you were saying to each other. Can I offer you my bedroom?'" Luca made his voice deeper to mimic Marco's.

Nina was drinking with gusto, and at each fresh bit of nonsense matched Luca's laughter with her own; she turned and gazed wide-eyed at Marco, to tease him about his drunken, addled expression. Again Luca bubbled over with laughter. A moment ago this laughter had been part of her own, the tone and rhythms fitting as though they had been made to measure; but this time it suddenly seemed ridiculous – the gaiety of a white wine, all froth and sparkle, seductive at the first sip and then disappointing. In a second the shrill elation died on her lips and in her eyes, and the bond of complicity with Luca snapped. With a sense of inner wonder, she suddenly recognized the same warm, frank gaze Marco had given her that morning long ago.

She felt bloated and drained. She wanted to touch him, to speak to him or to hear him speak, to feel him move beside her. The place, the time, and most of all Marco himself chimed in by an extraordinary chance with what she was thinking, and the lucky way that everything was in tune with her desires gave her a strange feeling of having stepped outside herself. Of all living beings he was the one with whom she found herself rubbing shoulders, and she breathed an emotion so intense it seemed to fill every instant. The word or gesture capable of expressing that fullness could only come of its own accord, as the waves rise out of the sea. She abandoned herself to Marco's gaze as to a word of love, feeling she must faint from the melting sensation in her arms and lips. But, as if it were nothing but a memory, her desire seemed condemned to a strange unreality; like a tree upside down, rooted in the air, her wonderment was clinging to something impossible, to that very losing of herself, so near and yet so far from him. Marco became aware of the change in Nina's expression; he saw her eyes locking with his in a secret communion, already questioning what it was he felt in his heart, begging him to reveal his thoughts, not to elude her, to love her immediately.

"Why ever don't you remember, Marco?" Nina's voice was not quite distinct now, either. Beneath the humorous note there was a hint of tears. Even in her body Marco no longer saw the angel from the world come to invite him to life. Her shapeliness seemed spoilt: the arms disproportionately long for the childlike hands, the chest already broad but the breasts still small. Her lips were smiling, but her eyes were far away, seeming to hasten on towards the horizon and the future. Intent as she was on taking refuge in childish mannerisms, or imitating those of a grown-up woman, when she found herself unmasked, when someone took her for what she really was, her act dissolved in a wail of fear and all she wanted was to weep and vanish. If only she could be alone now with Marco, and cease to share everything with Luca almost by instinct, as she had always done. She half closed her eyes, but the desire kept haunting her mind, so she tried to shrug it off by picking up the conversation.

"When you said 'I couldn't help overhearing you,' I thought 'What a gentleman. Is he Venetian?'" Nina said, turning to Marco but avoiding his eye.

"*Veneziani gran signori, Padovani gran dottori, Vicentini magnagatti, Veronesi tutti matti*," said Luca as if he were reciting some great epic. They all three laughed at his pompous tone of voice, and this gave Nina the break, the moment and the courage, to look Marco in the eye again. Marco felt assaulted by her look. He turned his head brusquely in Luca's direction, thinking he didn't much like this girl, didn't know who she was and didn't want to know. But he continued to feel her presence, as if thick clouds had rolled up over his head, threatening to burst over him in a storm.

"So you're Venetian?" asked Luca.

"No."

"Where were you born then?"

"In Trieste, but I was only born there. I've lived here and there."

"But why?" said Nina turning to him again. "Why ever didn't you want to stay in Trieste? How do you manage to leave everyone who loves you, and go and live somewhere where you don't know a soul, like a foreigner?" To give Nina an answer Marco would have had to feel sure of just what the hell he was doing and had done with his life. He was about to burst out with "What a question!" followed by a string of commonplaces spiced with details of journeys, experience acquired as a "citizen of the world". Instead he began to drum with two fingers on the table and sing ironically, "Here, where the whole world loves you, honest, loving and wise."

"*L'Elisir d'Amore*," said Luca instantly.

"Well done. Do you like opera?"

"Absolutely not."

"Oh come on now, that's like telling me you don't like the sun or the sea. Obviously you don't know it, or have never been taught to listen properly."

"You can't say that, I'm a musician. I've got a record of *L'Elisir*."

"And I'm a poet; I've got the *Divina Commedia* at home."

"No, truly," Nina interrupted. "He really is a good pianist."

"Fine, all the more reason. What about Verdi?"

"Um-cha-cha? No, I find the orchestrations too utterly boring."

"You're a case for prompt rescue, my lad. Otherwise who knows what ghastly music you'll produce." Now Marco was completely taken up with Luca and, warming to their discussion, he was saved from his stupor. He kept his eyes averted from Nina to avoid misunderstandings, but then he felt he had given too much importance to those glances, and looked at her with ostentatious indifference while talking with Luca, as if to say, "You see? We're not cutting you out. Or at least I'm not." But in her eyes he at once sensed the emotional intensity that he was trying to deny. Either he must keep his eyes to himself or say something serious.

Luca had only heard the most popular Verdi arias in the poorest possible recorded editions belonging to his father. With the help of Marco, who had prepared supper for them at his own flat, and was now explaining the conventions of the form and helping him to visualize the action on the stage, Luca was more than happy to give up those ill-founded prejudices.

Late that night Marco offered his bedroom to the young people for the second time, and took himself off to the study. As he looked at his books he felt an affinity with them: in the end, he told himself, there was nothing personal in his life. Relieved of the anguish which had constrained him to listen to Scarpa's pompous rhetoric and reduce his ideas to a size in keeping with such bombast, he felt free and unencumbered. He lay down fully dressed on the sofa, switched off the lamp and listened to the night's quiet in the distance outside his window.

He thought about Luca, such a receptive, open, lively lad, with such a promising future. Then he let his thoughts flow freely, but before he had a chance to recognize one idea, along came another, taking away the mental energy needed to think through the first. So the first idea would raise its voice and beat its fists on the table, insisting: "Think *me* now, then you can think about something else." But the racket it had raised was followed only by a moment's silence, and as soon as Marco tried to dedicate himself in a disciplined fashion to its demands he immediately found his thoughts split into channels like a river at its delta or like a schoolgirl without a teacher, interspersed only with some "whys" or "wherefores" which untangled the knots where the flow was interrupted. This confusion melted into a short sleep, from which he awoke thinking of Nina. He pictured her blue eyes, the softness of her hair, her translucent skin, her fine, pure brow and the delicate lines of her face. He was thinking of Nina, and of his not wanting to think of her, but by now the image of her was so intense that he knew he would not be able to sleep again, because she was in his bed, with Luca.

Then a seagull's cry, the happy whisperings of the young people, a short merry laugh like a splash of water, brought him back to his senses, restoring to him the thread of linear time. Silence, tangible silence. "Maybe they've fallen asleep," thought Marco. A long, sleepy sigh, followed by another, longer and deeper still. "That's Nina," he thought.

"Maybe she's asking for help." Nina's deep sighs tumbled out one upon another, and Marco stopped thinking and listened. As when one watches the rain falling and grows sad, the echo of Nina's pleasure, which sometimes seemed like a cry of pain, a call for help, flooded his mind and senses, as if those rains were swelling the river slowly, slowly, until the banks broke and it swept away the defence-less harvest.

Marco's mind was a blank. He tried to conjure up the figures who had helped his sentimental education; Julien, Don Alfonso, Romeo, Frédéric . . . but not one of them would come to his aid. All that came were the sighs of Luca and Nina, that sounded in his ears as an enhanced triviality racking him with solitude, with helplessness, with a longing for love; only those instants which had slipped past the guard of his intelligence and penetrated his heart like drunken vandals, drowning his thoughts with their hubbub. Those sighs were by now so violent that they filled the house and the scrap of sky enclosed within its walls. Marco held his throat in an effort to choke down the sob that rose as if his heart must burst from his chest, and stayed an instant frozen in that position, while Nina's ever-sharper cries sank into sobs, then silence.

Arid as the walls of the room, the sudden silence in which those kisses had been engulfed quickly cooled the intensity of his imagination. Just as the touch of sand – something at last not liquid – feels to a shipwrecked man, so the sensation of physical tiredness, the semi-darkness and the silence seemed all of a sudden wonderfully tangible to Marco, and the creations of his imagination crumbled into a peaceful sleep.

A calm, wordless smile lay on the lips of Nina and Luca, prophesying now and for ever that apart from that pleasure, the world is destructive, it divides into weeks and months, which are counted off one by one in the wasting away of time. That smile promised: "I will never free myself from your embrace, my love. The day will come to separate us, but come the evening I shall return to our embrace, even if I must search for you through all the world." And even if the day which was to separate them did not pass in a flash, as they hoped, but was the slow disintegration of their promise, they would return to that smile exchanged in silence, each alone in his own heart seeking that first embrace in which life had dawned, seeking the flavour of first love.

They crept out silently in the morning, carefully collecting their clothes, opening the door gently, whispering to each other, "Hurry, or we'll be late for school," tiptoeing so as not to wake Marco, who was still asleep in his clothes on the sofa. They left a note attached with a drawing-pin to the front door. Just "Goodbye and thank you. Nina and Luca." The cold wind that blew in their faces seemed to be saying "You should have stayed in bed, my little ones." It set the tone for the day: school, lunch with their respective parents, respectively sullen, an afternoon spent studying, the night alone, divided and in separate beds, an insufferable outlook, a day to be written off from the outset. They had coffee in the bar opposite the school, watching the gloomy grey faces of their schoolfellows and teachers, who filed through the main doorway as if into a church where a funeral was going on, lending a touch of the macabre to the morning.

"Oh curse it," whispered Nina, her mouth buried in her cup.

"Hurry up, it's time," answered Luca, and together they crossed the threshold of the school.

During the last few months of lower school the clash between Scarpa and the fourth form got worse, partly because seeing his pupils grow up, leaving his class and eventually the school, filled Scarpa with rage, for it made him feel like a dog chained to the job of teaching. Partly too, because a teacher's reputation in the school is formed largely by the dozen or so of his students who fail to pass and are forced to go through another year with him, to "lose a year", as it is so aptly termed. Now that class too, thanks to desperate study, were about to escape him.

But because the senior Italian teacher was retiring, Scarpa had been offered the course in Italian literature in the higher grades, so that Nina and Luca, having previously endured him in the guise of inquisitor in nouns and verbs, now found themselves saddled with him as he unfolded Dante and Petrarch.

That morning, as was his wont, the teacher entered the class with the register tucked firmly under his arm. He swept a satisfied eye over the cemetery of frightened faces he had managed to create in his class, and began the ritual by which he invested himself with power before them. Even now, ten years after his degree, he couldn't help reminding himself for a moment before starting class with a self-satisfied smirk, that he was a doctor of literature and philosophy.

"Well, girls and boys, tell me what you have made of this poem of Dante's," he said, sounding a false note of benevolence, tenderly recalling the time when, as a schoolboy himself, he had been sweetly innocent of the subject of literature. His students confirmed his supposition by preserving a unanimous silence. Only a few had read the poem, and those few held opinions differing so widely from his that keeping their mouths shut seemed preferable to a discussion in which the teacher was bound to get irritable, and, as like as not, to punish them. In fact Scarpa had no patience with other people's ideas or opinions about literature, least of all those of his pupils, since he was himself entirely deficient in this field. Having savoured these delicious minutes of his pupils' submission, Scarpa settled down to study the register, the only text he had ever truly studied, and basically the only part of his profession he cared about.

"Brandi, would you start by reading and commenting on the first few lines of the poem?" he asked most civilly, as if Luca were in any position to answer, "No, sir, I don't feel like it this morning."

> "Tanto gentile e tanto onesta pare
> la donna mia quand'ella altrui saluta,
> ch'ogni lingua deven tremando muta
> e li occhi no l'ardiscon di guardare."

"That's enough. Now repeat these concepts in your own words, please."

"What concepts, sir?"

"That's what I'm asking you: what concepts?"

"Personally, I don't think there are any concepts. If I say it in my own words, I'll ruin the rhythm, and the sense, and the result will be so banal . . ."

"First of all," Scarpa interrupted, "we are at school, not in the theatre. I asked you to repeat it in your own words, so would you kindly do so and not contradict me. I have my reasons, but if you are so retarded as not to see them, I shall have to explain. It is of no importance whether you like the poem or not. I want to see if you can express yourself, and know how to paraphrase."

"But if you paraphrase the lines you destroy them. Beatrice's footsteps are in the rhythm."

"Go ahead and destroy them then, Brandi," Scarpa interrupted him again, not wanting to give him a chance to say things he had not asked for, perhaps gleaned from some book which was foreign to him. No, Brandi was to answer the question, however stupid it might be. At least that way he would learn his place. Luca gave a discontented snort, then, calculating the risk he ran by angering the teacher, began to recite in a quibbling, toneless voice:

"My lady seems so gentle and modest when she greets others that every tongue becomes mute, trembling, and the eyes have no courage to look at her."

"Good. Now let's pretend you're Dante. What adjective would you use instead of 'mute'?"

"Mute."

"You wouldn't be having me on, Brandi?"

"No, sir. I think the choice of word is right, and there's no point in my pretending to be Dante, because Dante existed, and 'mute' is what he said. This is a silly exercise."

"How dare you! Are you trying to teach me?"

"I don't want to teach anybody anything."

"Well stop it at once, I say. You are continually interrupting me, and I can't waste the whole lesson on you. Sit down. Ferri, please continue from where your fellow-pupil left off to give us a lesson."

Ferri took over the reading, while Scarpa simmered down slightly. Come to think of it, he rather liked what Brandi had said about Beatrice's footsteps being in the rhythm of the thing. A bite crude, of course, but dressed up a little it could at the very least fill in time. And then, who knows? It was just one of the little things he had heard along the way, and maybe one day he'd settle down and make a collection of these filched ideas . . . Meanwhile Ferri had stopped reading, and the class was waiting in silence for something to happen. Let them wait, Scarpa said to himself. He took two or three turns up and down among the desks, collecting his thoughts, then went back to his desk, gazed into space, and began:

"What the poet says seems to me sufficiently clear without my explaining it. I think we can say . . . yes, I think we can say . . . that this is an expressionistic poem. It expresses, I think we can say – as your honoured fellow-pupil tried to explain, albeit in a confused way – absolutely what it wants to express in the very way in which it expresses it, if you will forgive me the play on words."

At this point, we will spare the reader the speculations, the true and false anecdotes concerning the life of the poet, the teacher's deliberate and accidental wordplay on the poem. His feeble-minded histrionic style was just sending the whole class sweetly to sleep when Scarpa, suddenly changing his tone of voice, concluded his explanation.

"Therefore, the poem should be read in the following manner:

"Tàanto gentìile e tàanto onèesta pàare
La dòonna mìia quand'èella altrùui salùuta."

Scarpa re-read the whole poem at an exasperating snail's pace, with long pauses between lines, and accentuating all the unimportant words as if he were reading in a language he didn't know.

"Do you understand, Brandi? Come out here now, right here in front of me, and read the whole thing again."

Luca closed the book with a cocksure gesture, left his desk, and recited the poem from memory in front of the class. If Scarpa had succeeded in making those lines sound pedestrian with his explanations and his ridiculous reading, Luca succeeded in giving them life again, speaking the lines without affectation, without overstressing the rhyme or the metre.

"Good, see how much better you're reciting it. Why, you nearly know it by heart."

78

"No thanks to your explanation, sir."

"What an insolent, presumptuous puppy you are!"

Luca saw the trembling of Scarpa's lip, which generally heralded one of his outbursts, and instinctively took a step backwards. Scarpa had followed Luca word by word in the book, hoping to catch him out in a mistake, but, put on the spot again by Luca's easy mastery, he found his hands clenching and unclenching with rage.

"That will do, Brandi. Go back to your place. Evidently all my years of study, my school finals, which all of you still have to face, and, if you ever get there, a university degree – and I can assure you that in my day it wasn't the walkover it is now – have done me no good at all. Along comes Signor Brandi to explain to me how Dante should be read! Excellent, excellent, very good indeed. We live and learn."

He dragged these words out slowly and as he attempted to recover his ironical tone of voice, they had an engaging aptness. He stressed the words *finals* and *Signor* Brandi in an attempt to regain his swagger, which was somewhat unsteady this morning. The sound of the bell released him from the embarrassment of rounding off his peroration. For once, his pupils would have preferred to remain in class, to see what lesson he would draw from his conclusion.

6

Another afternoon, another evening, another night. Another winter's or another summer's day. "Come along, Nina, serving up!" Looking through the window in static moments of grey listlessness, fixed dead as nails in a wall. Moving like some aged animal from bed to table, table to bed. Another day. And another. "Dinner's ready." At table no one speaks. What is there to say? It's not possible. It's unbearable. It's death. "What's bugging you?" one might say, or simply "Bye-bye then." Another hour, then evening and a phone call to Luca. Night. Sleep.

Sometimes come thoughts of the future, the summer, some great scheme. "Nothing, it doesn't matter. It's not important, forget it." Better to vanish completely, like smoke dissolving in air, like words which have no meaning. "Dinner's ready, Nina." "I'm coming."

Sometimes there is rain. The gutter ticks like a clock. Or someone is walking overhead. Or the children in the flat below are yelling again – this time someone's hurt himself. Time passes as if flushed down the lavatory, it seems, without letting itself be lived. Learn up a few pages, what a bore. In spring the birds return and make their nests. Sundays one can sleep. "Serving up, Nina." "I'm coming." "Have you finished already?" "Yes." "You never say anything." Who never says anything? And anyway, who says?

"I'm s'posed to be swotting, aren't I? I'll telephone Luca first, though. Luca's out, damn him, he must be at Marco's again this evening." "Nina, it's ready." "I'm coming." But haven't we already eaten? Perhaps that was yesterday. Or perhaps yesterday is already tomorrow. "Nina!" "I'm coming, I'm coming."

That flat, which her father had made his lair, his refuge from the street and from people, shrank for Nina and grew more constricted and uncomfortable every day. Year after year, the noises that reached her from the canalside through her open window, the afternoon light and even the rain seemed to sing of a happiness from which she was cut off by those walls; they held her prisoner in a limbo divorced from sexuality and from ageing, an absurd extension of her puberty. She hated everything and everyone and only wanted to escape. Sometimes she felt she ought to rebel, but against what? What stifled her had no name; it was the sameness permeating the walls, the narrowness of the horizon of her surroundings, the few, threadbare words spoken by her parents, the fact of being trapped with them in a single destiny.

Her father had shut himself off from the world with a scowl, and had laid the responsibility for his silence on Maria and Nina. There were no whys or wherefores: he had to work, keep the place on its feet. To justify himself for the gloom he had imposed on the household he had sacrificed one after another the few pleasures he had previously allowed himself: football on the television, the glass of wine after work, sugar in his coffee. In this way he evened the score, if ever they felt inclined to take issue with him.

And he was afraid. Every day more afraid. He was an assiduous reader of the crime pages and the obituaries and, feeling himself threatened even in that tiny corner of the planet where he had taken refuge with his household, he had fortified the flat with bolts and chains, bars on the windows and even an alarm system which was certainly worth more than anything there was to steal inside. Crossing the city each day was terribly wearisome, populated as it was (he felt) entirely by rapists, muggers, and murderers – a place full of disasters and plagues. After supper, he'd collapse in front of the televison, muttering, "Holy Mother of God, what times we live in! There isn't a decent soul left in the world."

Caught between Pietro's neurotic isolation and Nina's boredom was Maria, an involuntary loner, with no role in life and practically no place to call her own. She'd try talking first with one and then with the other, but was always left feeling that she'd said the wrong thing or was being a bore – better to keep quiet, then, so as not to make things worse.

One evening after supper, as Pietro was leaving the table to return to his discontented mutterings in front of the television news, she let slip an "Oh, shit!", an expression which she had always banned in her house, along with similar ones: "We don't say that," she would remark, or "that's not nice" – comments that epitomized her submission to the rules of respectability. Pietro didn't hear, or pretended not to hear, but Nina started to giggle. Encouraged by that laugh, Maria began telling her the most pathetic details about her marriage, of which Nina had had no notion; the girl could not help feeling somewhat sympathetic.

A little at a time, during the long conversation between mother and daughter as they cleared the table and washed the dishes, in those moments of the daily routine from which (and now they understood why) Pietro had been banished, Maria found the courage to lament her loneliness, the kisses vanished into the wilful silence of her man, the intimacy in which she had lived for so long and which had little by little evaporated. She wept over the shyness, the embarrassment she felt undressing in front of Pietro these days, as if she were an intruder; she regretted the smiles she no longer knew what to do with, though they occasionally sprang again to her lips like a flash-back, the reflux of past happiness. For now her nights with Pietro – with her saying, "What's up, friend?" and his inevitable rejoinder, "Let me get to sleep, Maria, please, you know I've got to work tomorrow, and don't suppose I like it" – certainly gave her little to laugh about.

These conversations came to an immediate halt when Pietro entered the kitchen. Maria quickly dried her eyes, and, having spent the past two hours tearing strips off him, resumed her mask of submission, and asked him, "Did you need something, Pietro?" With all the sacrifices he made for the family, Pietro did not imagine that his womenfolk could have any complaints about him and, muttering under his breath, he went back to the television.

Nina was surprised at the childish quality of her mother's comments, at the kinds of thing that amused her, and at the fact that she knew the names of every one of Nina's schoolfellows without having met any of them except Luca. She could not help comparing her mother's life with her own possible future, in which the achievement of maturity might be utterly denied her by the unending male dominance. She shuddered at the thought.

At the end of Nina's second year at her present school, Maria's mother came to live with them. She had taken a fancy to Luca, and said to Nina: "What a good-looking lad. Be careful he doesn't go queer on you." And she cackled, without even herself knowing why, at the word "queer", at its exaggerated familiarity, at Nina's amazement. She had immediately felt at home with the two women of the household while Pietro, on the other hand, especially with all that array of useless anti-theft devices, she had found a continual irritant. "Look at all these bolts and bars – they're a load of balls! What do you think they are going to steal, you ninny – your cock?"

Nina became extremely fond of her. Even the signs of physical decay in her grandmother seemed endowed with a special charm – the vagaries of her memory, her stoutness, her deafness, to which anyway she did not admit, thereby involuntarily achieving a somewhat surrealistic genius for answering unasked questions, or grabbing the wrong end of the stick. Through her grandmother Nina entered briefly into contact with a marvellous society – that of elderly women who had outlived their husbands – which her grandmother frequented regularly to have a good gossip. The dignified life of that little group of people on the way out – people who lived among rusty outworn conventions and were either patronized or regarded as nostalgic throwbacks, and indeed treated with impatience, or worse, with the implicitly apologetic tones of those who consider the elderly only in terms of their approaching demise – taught Nina much about what it means to be on the edge of life, grimly holding on to the last remnants of their identity.

Michele Scarpa and his followers had moved to a new bar in the Cannaregio district.

"Our reunions," he preached, "are not only a way of passing the time; we are the guinea-pigs in an exploration of new social relationships."

The exploration of new social relationships carried him back to bed with Marina, who was, aside from Beniamino Bortoletti, the greatest admirer of his qualities. Companions in both school and university, Marina and Michele had already come together and separated a dozen times, the results in both cases, of inertia rather than of initiative. Michele had never thought much of her, and in leaving her he had always expatiated on the inevitable disparity between individuals, how in the long run it was hardly his fault if he was more sensitive and intelligent than she was. This had been his conclusion each time as he left her without a word of farewell, secure in the knowledge that his position in the group would keep her at his beck and call; he didn't even notice the regularity with which he went back to her.

In this umpteenth loveless encounter, which had followed her break with Marco Invancich, certain new features arose to change the balance between the pair. Michele, at the age of thirty-nine, felt the time had come to stop living with his parents, and moved in with Marina. "Oh the shame of it, the shame of it!" wailed his mother and threatened never to see him again, to disinherit him, before redressing the balance by offering them an apartment and a considerable sum of money to help them set up house. After a brief and feeble resistance, which very soon began to look like haggling, Michele decided on marriage and told Marina the news. A few weeks later they tied the knot in a little church on the mainland. Michele had made Marina swear to tell nobody about the wedding, and it was precisely this fear of discovery which convinced her she should marry him. More than any other consideration, it was the weakness Michele had shown, first with his mother and now with her, which persuaded her that this marriage was to her advantage. In the prevarication, the bribery, the shame that had influenced Michele's choice, Marina realized the importance of the family for him. She came to see that in marrying him she would gain enormous power over him, so she accepted the apartment and the money Michele's parents had offered so disinterestedly, and accepted him as well, in the complete assurance that by so doing she would not lose one jot of her freedom.

The religious ceremony was swift and painless for both of them. Michele didn't even listen to what the priest was saying, and Marina was amused. She now had the upper hand and she let him know immediately – already in the very first days, beneath her polite exterior, Michele was aware of a strange arrogance in her, but paid little attention to it. He allowed himself to be led along by the situation, becoming ever more weak-willed, both in his dealings with her, and in his own solitary thoughts, where the incongruity between his principles and what he had become was beginning to show.

Michele spent the first months of their married life in a strange bewilderment. He attempted more or less to preserve his old habits about the house, which saddled his attendant female with all the daily duties: to her fell the job of cleaning the house as also that of keeping affection warm, however little reliance he placed on it – far from it, he took pleasure in sneering as he indulged in his feeble sermons, at school and at the café, on the society of the future.

But Marina, who was getting to know him better and better, was now always a jump ahead of him in such matters. By comparing the two worlds she managed to dominate both of them; she easily located the subjects evaded in daily life and then watched their grotesque transformation into ideology. Every day, with cutting observations and poisonous remarks whispered in his ear like love-words or flung across the table during conversations among friends, while leaning on his arm to ensure his complicity, she forced him to become one of the herd, the role he had always consigned to his faithful followers. The future, Michele had always believed, would one day, sooner or later, turn itself to his advantage and, by extension, to the advantage of his kind; for the moment it alarmed him; no matter how hard he tried to project himself into the dimension which for so long had allowed him to be blind to his way of life, all he saw before him now was the endless repetition of exactly what oppressed him: Marina for ever, school for ever, that house, that city, that Michele for ever! To give a political-social-cosmic-economical-cultural analysis in the café had become almost impossible with Marina around; his own weaknesses prevented his attacking the weaknesses of others; he preferred not to listen, not to speak; to drink his coffee and pretend he wasn't there.

However, it was at home that life was most intolerable. Marina forced him to admit to the high-handed way he had treated his uncomplaining mother, and now that he had occasionally to wash a plate or make the bed, the chains which he had so often prated on about were well and truly clamped around his wrists; nor would anyone come to loosen them. So he attempted a sudden volte-face.

"Marina, our love is deeper than I can express; I have learnt so much from being with you that I feel I know what I want in life. Let's have a baby, let's give some meaning to our future."

"You must be mad. If we have a baby, or rather if I have a baby, because you, my sweet, will have very little to do with it, that'll be no future – it'll be the end. Changing nappies all the time, and penny-pinching, we'll turn into one of those pathetic ex-revolutionary couples."

"But what meaning does it have, then? What do you want from me?"

"What meaning do you expect it to have? We've got a house, we make love, we've interests in common . . ."

Marina was talking as Michele would have done had he not married her. During the conversation, they measured each other up, trying to judge how much hypocrisy they could permit themselves. Michele talked of love, which for him was little more than a pretext. Marina latched on to the word revolution, for which she found a temporary use, purely in order to keep the vice firmly clamped on Michele's life and measure the ground she had gained over him in these first months. And it was a great deal: he was already prepared to play traitor to his friends in the café, if only to achieve a little peace in the daily household wrangle. Thus Michele abandoned the cardboard throne from which he had instructed everybody what they should think, say and do, at home and abroad. He was possessed by a continual uncertainty, the reasons for which were now beyond his control, for in point of fact they were all in Marina's hands.

Each night she listened to his monotonous confession as he pulled the fabric of his personality to pieces, demolished his youthful illusions, admitted insecurity, weakness, fear. Michele spoke for hours, and these days only to her, without realizing what she was like, equally surprised by a kind word or a cruel one, and hoping that since she had fallen to his lot as a wife she understood and loved him. But he was so unaccustomed to paying any attention to human beings other than himself, or even noticing their existence, that his observations of her character failed to make any coherent sense. Eventually, unable to think of what to say, he discharged himself haphazardly of scraps of sincerity muddled together with verbal traps into which he was fatally bound to fall himself.

The only place where Scarpa's power had not passed into Marina's hands was the school. "I don't have great ideas any more," he thought to himself, "but here, who can get at me?" Freed at last from the onerous task of being an intellectual, he could give free reign to his bullying tendencies: unexpected tests, fail-marks galore. With only a few months to go till the end of the school year, everyone taking his courses was assured of failure.

The final-year students, among whom were Luca and Nina, let off steam one day with their science teacher, an old member of the Fourth International, and the only one of the teaching staff who felt any sympathy for them.

"He's crazy the way he comes down on us," said Ferri. "He must be off his chump. If we don't do something about it they won't even let us sit our exams."

"There's nothing we *can* do," interrupted Robazza in his usual lugubrious tone. "He's holding all the cards."

"But it's crazy, absolutely crazy, Signora. You know what he did yesterday?" Ferri went on, warming to his theme. "He asked us about a poem he hadn't even set us, one of Foscolo's. Every time someone didn't answer, a two just like that! And it wasn't even a set poem. That's just plain nuts!"

"It'll have to go through the school board," the teacher said, trying to play things down.

"The next lesson we have," put in Nina, "we won't even answer the roll-call, we'll clam up for the whole hour. In any case, it doesn't make any difference to *him* any more whether we're there or not."

"But it's crazy," objected Ferri. "That way we'll only get given a whole lot more twos. We've got to scare him. Let's put a bomb in his house!"

The class burst out laughing at this bright idea of Ferri's, but after a short discussion decided to adopt Nina's plan.

The next day Scarpa entered the classroom, put down the register on the front desk of the middle row, counted the absentees but didn't tick them off, laid the register with an impatient gesture on the teacher's desk behind him and began stalking to and fro between the desks, as was his habit. He would call the roll from behind their backs, and expect them to answer the empty teacher's chair. He conceived of his own authority as an abstract thing these days, no longer connected with his person but with the school, with society at large. This allowed him to engage more freely in his favourite activity, that of playing police-man: to find the textbook for the next lesson open on the desk, to detect a note, a giggle, an expression, a nod, a glance . . . That morning his pupils sat absolutely motionless, offering him no chance to let fly at them with his usual punishments, or his "What is there to laugh about? Out with it, let's share the joke," followed by the allocation of a mark that just about summed up the amount of Italian literature his students would ever learn from *him*. Faced with the embarrassing alternative of starting a lesson which he hadn't prepared, he waited ten minutes, pacing to and fro with mounting impatience, watching for someone to make the move which would enable him to get up to his old tricks. He rubbed his hands at the thought that if he wished he could remain silent for the whole hour, read the paper, think his own thoughts, condemn them to the most appalling boredom, and nobody would be able to raise the slightest objection. But after a while the unusual intensity of the silence irked him.

"What's the matter with you all this morning?" he burst out. "You're so dead quiet there must be something brewing. Have you lost your tongues? Very well, let's see if you get them back when I call out the roll. Antoni. Answer me: what's the matter with you this morning? Very well, Antoni, two out of ten. Brandi? Aha, you have also taken a vow of silence? Well done, well done. A two for you as well. Cinti? Contin? Degan?"

His pupils, mute and impassive, heard the professor's fury mounting with each name. The roll-call over, Scarpa solemnly closed the register, raked them with his eyes and yelled: "This isn't the end of the matter, I can tell you."

He went to the door and began to squawk, "Porter, here, Porter." The porter came hurrying up, and Scarpa asked him to call the headmaster. Scarpa repeated the roll-call in front of the headmaster. His pupils repeated their silence.

"This is the second time they have refused to answer,

headmaster, sir. It would seem that they've all lost their tongues."

"Boys and girls, it is your duty to answer your teacher," the headmaster said, giving each word the full weight of authority.

"Can we suspend the whole class? Refuse to let them sit their exam?" urged Scarpa.

"Certainly we can. Indeed, if this behaviour continues we shall be forced to do so."

"Please, sir," said Nina, getting to her feet; "please would you take a look at the register?" Headmaster and teacher stood for a moment as if turned to stone, disconcerted by Nina's determined tone of voice. "Please do, sir," Nina repeated, holding the venerable headmaster's eye. Scarpa froze. Suddenly it flashed before him what a pass he had come to in his profession; and he knew for certain that he was in the wrong. He was assailed by the intense, confused sense of regret which, ever since marrying Marina and admitting to his own incoherence, had plagued and tormented him. Now it caught in his throat like a sob and he felt his voice disappear down into his throat, there in front of the headmaster, and in full view of his pupils, who sat in a huddle among the desks like a gigantic pile of dirty dishes waiting to be washed. He realized that he had to say something to the headmaster, to convince him that he had the situation under control, would never let a pupil – and a female into the bargain – take the initiative; but instead he felt catapulted into their midst, as if he were one of the victims, one of those pupils he had always managed to crush under his heel, but who had now sprung up like an insidious weed. How could he have let it happen? The suspicion that, by calling the headmaster to examine the fruits of his neurosis, he had laid this trap with his own hands, filled him with terror.

The headmaster, aware that he should waste no time, moved towards the teacher's desk and made as if to open the register. But Scarpa, with a desperate, instinctive movement, put his elbow on it, and whispered in a sickly, plaintive manner, "Oh sir, surely you are not going to listen to these good-for-nothings. You will put my professional standing in jeopardy."

The headmaster, with the ghost of a smile, jerked the register from under Scarpa's elbow, and whispered menacingly, "What are you afraid of, Dr Scarpa?"

He needed no reply to this question, for it was all written there before him in the register. The perfectly uniform column of twos out of ten, which Scarpa in his fury had assigned even to two pupils absent that morning, and the disastrous display of that term's marks, were explanation enough.

"Their marks are catastrophic, as you can see," Scarpa began in an apologetic voice. "There isn't a single one of them, not one, who remembers the grammar we have studied, none of them can read a poem properly, not one of them has a whit of feeling for literature. They are complete layabouts, sir, I promise you. If you only knew what they get up to instead of studying. You just can't imagine what hell these years have been. We must fail the lot of them, not allow them to sit their exams. Otherwise, what are we here for? We surely don't want to become their laughing-stock. We don't come in here, dear children, morning after morning, merely to be parodied in your pornographic caricatures." And, turning to the headmaster, "Do you know what these young beggars get up to, sir? Look at these! I confiscated them the other morning."

Scarpa opened a drawer which he kept locked, and pulled out a pathetic little bundle of caricatures. The headmaster was particularly shaken by a drawing depicting himself, sticking his bum out towards an unidentified phallus protruding from a scrimmage of teachers.

"Bravo!" exclaimed the headmaster. "So this is what you've learnt to do in five years."

"Please, sir," Nina interrupted, still on her feet, "I don't know what the teacher is showing you, but whatever it is it's not the point."

"Not the point?" shouted Scarpa. "See if *this* isn't the point." And he thrust another caricature under her nose. Nina recognized it as the work of Robazza, and sat down without further comment. The headmaster, meanwhile, had arranged the drawings in some order on the desk and was examining them closely.

"Who did these drawings? Come on, speak up. Who did them?" he said, having finally come to the conclusion that they were all done by the same hand.

"They're all to blame, sir, every one of them," Scarpa protested angrily.

"That is not so. These drawings have a single author, and we shall now discover who it is."

Scarpa had barricaded himself behind his desk, convinced that his problems were over, still growling "It's all of them, the whole lot of them," at that mass of heads he could still scarcely tell apart after five years. How could he have thought for a single moment that the headmaster would not back him up? Now the two of them would put the brats in their places and give them a proper hiding.

Just then Robazza stood up, and in his usual lugubrious voice said, "It was me, sir. The teacher confiscated them from me back in the junior school."

"Is this true, Scarpa?" asked the headmaster, taken aback. "Why did you not take disciplinary action at the time? How can we punish him now, for drawings he did five years ago?"

"It's a lie, sir," Michele said. But his tone of voice betrayed such dismay that even had he said "My name is Michele Scarpa," there would have been reason to doubt him. The headmaster looked at Robazza. An embarrassing situation indeed. However, a lesson was called for. He must stand up against the determined solidarity of the students with equal vigour. Otherwise he would become an accomplice to Scarpa's weakness.

"Very well, Robazza," he said, with extreme coldness, "this time you have gone beyond all bounds. A laugh is a laugh, as long as it is a joke, but these drawings reveal a squalor and turpitude of mind that I cannot overlook. I ought to call the police, and get you packed off to an institution more suited to your type . . ."

To remember those caricatures had already been humiliating enough for Robazza. Now the threat of such a punishment, so far out of proportion to the crime, chilled him to the marrow, but what could he do about it?

"So," continued the headmaster, "you will now proceed to remove your books, your coat and yourself, and go back to wherever you came from, because from this moment on you are no longer a pupil in this school. I don't suppose, however, that this will be any great loss to *you*, since in this school we study *humanitas*, and not *animalium mores*." The headmaster was alone in laughing at the quip, and threw an ugly glance at Scarpa, who couldn't for the life of him understand the joke. Robazza remained seated and grasped his chair.

"Come along now, did you not understand what I said? Do you want me to repeat it in swinish? Or do you want me to call the police? You are expelled from this school! Your school year is at an end. Think how many beautiful drawings you'll have time for now!"

Robazza collected his books and his coat and moved

towards the door, casting an appealing look at the head-master, begging the man to revoke his decision and let him take his diploma, with the exams only a month or two away. The boy was soon through the door, but a moment later he stuck his head back in and shouted: "If there's a swine in here you can be sure it's not me, sir!" And he slammed the door behind him.

Scarpa, in raptures over the sharp and effective lesson which the headmaster had just given the class, and feeling sure of himself again, exclaimed: "What infernal insolence. They get above themselves!"

"What do you mean, Scarpa?"

Nina rose to her feet and, picking up her things, left the room, followed immediately by Luca.

"I warn you all not to leave this room," Scarpa admonished the rest of the class, but his tone of voice was enough to persuade even the most hesitant – they rose up from their desks and followed Nina and Luca into the corridor. The headmaster and Scarpa gazed in bewilderment at the empty classroom.

"When you have concluded the lesson," the headmaster said, turning with some embarrassment to Scarpa, "please come for a moment to my office and bring that register."

"But sir, the matter is closed, isn't it? As you can see very well for yourself, there is no one left to teach. To whom shall I give my lesson?"

"I don't want to hear about that, Scarpa. I'll see you at the end of the hour."

In the corridor the students were huddled together around Robazza, talking in an excited hubbub of voices.

"Don't worry, Robazza, if they won't let you come back to school they won't see a single one of us either."

"Never again." "They can't treat us like dirt." "What a bastard!" "Couple of bastards if you ask me." "Crazy!"

"What d'you mean, crazy! It's the kind of thing they *would* do." "No, it's crazy. We'll blow the whole place up with a bomb, it's the only way, even if it seems crazy." "What the fuck are you talking about? It needs more than a bomb. We must think of something." "Yeah! Like keeping our mouths shut for the whole lesson, maybe? Look where that's got us!" "At least it was an idea." "You're crazy." "Let's meet at the Zattere this afternoon." "Four o'clock?" "O.K, I'll get the bomb ready in any case." "Great, Ferri. Might come in useful." "Oh shut up about bombs, will you." "You're all off your heads."

The headmaster came up to the group and the chatter ceased.

"I should like you to bear in mind that Robazza alone has been expelled. I shall expect the rest of you to come to school tomorrow, and we shall see what can be done about your marks in Italian, to enable you to take your final exams."

The school day had ended. They all left together, still repeating, "Four o'clock, then?" "Mind you're there too, Robazza." "We're going to make life pretty hard for them." "Four o'clock, then." "O.K, four o'clock."

Alone in the classroom, during the handful of minutes in which the headmaster had suggested he should teach the walls, Scarpa reviewed his profession. What had led him of all people to become a teacher, seeing that for him every idea was a small step forward in the pursuit of power over others? How ever could he have got himself trapped in a situation like this one, where he had no idea of what to do or say? And why was he now so scared at being summoned to the headmaster's study, just like a schoolboy? Ah well, he thought to himself, if there were a reason for everything, I would never have got married, so there are some questions it's pointless to ask.

Notwithstanding this, however, the incident did bring some simple truths home to him. He found himself involuntarily thinking of his students, of his own blunders, rather than the reasons for what had occurred; and being unable to distract his mind from these undoubtedly counter-productive thoughts, he tried to ridicule them in the hope that sarcasm might absolve him from responsibility: "Behaving as if we were equals. The dignity of the pupil, indeed! Why don't they go home to their mummies, have a good cry and forget about it by tomorrow? What they're short of is guts not sympathy. No one can deny that I've studied, taken my degree, got my teacher's diploma . . . must be worth something, all that. If not, then we're surrounded by a bunch of fools! And that old imbecile of a headmaster – he can go to the devil too! I look after his students every morning for him, don't I? He should count himself lucky."

He tried to find himself witty, but he scarcely felt amused. The time had come for him to go to the headmaster and give a convincing explanation of his behaviour. When the bell rang he had mentally prepared some kind of defence, and felt almost calm.

In the secretary's office, as he waited to be summoned into the presence, he fiddled idly with a button on his jacket, trying desperately to keep his mind off the fact that he totally lacked any convincing argument to justify himself before the headmaster.

"May I say one thing before you speak," Scarpa began at once, on being ushered into the headmaster's study, assuming a light-hearted manner. "May I congratulate you, sir, on the lesson you gave me today? The scope and complexity of the responsibilities inherent in our profession have never been so clearly demonstrated to me. The same goes for the role played by the school, and all other public institutions of our society. I said to myself, Michele, you see now what a lot you have to learn before you can even think of applying for a headship. Indeed, since I have been at this school, I have never witnessed such a display of strength and firmness – of courage, I might say – and at the same time, if you will permit me, of extreme simplicity, as indeed all great things are essentially simple."

"Thank you, thank you, *Dottore* Scarpa. Do take a seat. Speaking of the incident concerning that wretch Robazza, I certainly cannot admit to feeling any pride there. Had I not found myself faced with a set of rebels and a young promising teacher such as yourself – and I notice that you are not unobservant – I should have seen the whole matter in quite a different light. You know as well as I do that poor Robazza is paying more heavily than he should for his sketching."

"If you say so, sir, I cannot but agree with you."

"Thank you, thank you, Scarpa. Now where were we?" mused the headmaster. Victim of an excess of senile vanity, he lost the thread whenever he was paid a compliment, or even only spoken to, for he interpreted everything as a compliment, however vague and indirect.

"Ah yes, of course, 3B. So, I see you have understood, my dear Scarpa, that the point under discussion is quite another. We must not allow the students to throw doubt upon the prestige of the teaching staff."

"No possibility of that while you are our backbone and our guide."

"Thank you, thank you, Scarpa. In any case, discipline and professional ability are inextricably linked in this job. I acted as I did in order to avoid unpleasant repercussions. *Si vis pacem para bellum*. You understand me if I speak Latin, do you not?"

"Of course, of course," Scarpa answered, nodding vigorously. The headmaster's vanity provided a possible way out of his trouble. It seemed as if in that stream of adulation, some unknown genie had come to his aid, especially now that he'd run short of excuses. He smiled, and thought that everything was going to turn out for the best. Maybe in the end the headmaster would actually be congratulating him for one reason or another, just to make the peace.

"Don't you worry, sir. If I find myself faced with another case of insubordination I shall know what to do."

"Excellent, excellent, Scarpa. I like to see you so zealous."

"With such a backing . . ."

"Please don't mention it – however, thank you, thank you."

"You have nothing to thank *me* for. The credit is entirely yours. I have done nothing but bear witness to it, and anybody would say the same."

"Oh come now, we mustn't exaggerate. However, it was something else I wanted to speak to you about," the headmaster continued, without altering his tone of voice, and making a vast effort to shift his attention away from those intoxicating eulogies. "Tell me, are your pupils really such a wash-out in Italian literature? You know, what kind of impression are we going to make in front of the school commissioners, the parents, if the class is presented to them with an average of four out of ten? After all, you've had them all these years and you haven't even taught them to write properly!"

The headmaster's voice was still friendly, so much so that Michele didn't realize where the questions were leading. Taken in by this affability, he leaned back in his chair and began to speak in a relaxed, feckless manner.

"I know myself that it seems quite incredible, my dear sir, but not a single one of them can write a blessed essay in Italian as it should be written."

Then the full meaning of the question suddenly dawned on him, and he continued hastily: "No . . . er, that is . . .

I mean to say their progress is very poor, perhaps more in oral than in written work. Or vice versa. In some cases, that is . . . In any case, those marks should not be taken at face value."

"This is an official document, you know that, Scarpa. What's written is written. If you have to take disciplinary measures, there is the class register, and any number of more immediate and effective methods – such as the one you saw me employ this morning."

"I have learnt a great deal today, believe me."

"No doubt, Scarpa, but stick to the point. What standard have these children reached? Am I to believe the register? Am I to believe what you're saying to me now? What do you suggest?"

"Well, as I have said, it's a poor standard, as the register shows, but if . . ."

"But if what?" interrupted the headmaster. "Haven't you just this minute told me these marks should not be taken at face value? You are contradicting yourself, sir."

Michele was silent. He had begun to fiddle with the button again, and had understood much more from the headmaster's sudden change of tone than from what he had actually said so far.

"I think perhaps it would be better if I myself came tomorrow morning to test the children. You seem to me tired, my dear Scarpa. Being in charge of young people for five years is no mean task. Why don't you take a break? We can find you a stand-in for a few months – let's say until the exams. And at the beginning of the next school year we will reconsider. What do you say to that?"

Michele blanched. Was he to be thrown out of here too? Where would he go? What would he tell Marina? How could he face an extra five hours a day with her? And what repercussions would such an absence have on his career?

Lost in these thoughts he had almost forgotten he was in the headmaster's study, absorbed in the fate of that button on his coat and knowing it would soon come off. But there he was, and he had to say something.

"Let me try again. I think I have understood . . ."

"No, Scarpa. I have already made a promise to the youngsters. I advise you, in your own interests, to step down. Can you imagine the scandal there would be if people found out what you've been doing to the register in a city such as ours, where, without either boasting or false modesty, we may say that this school holds a top position? The newspapers would get hold of it – Heavens alive! there would be slogans all over the walls, as in '68. I can't even bear to think of it. And now, if you have nothing further to say to me, I must ask you to leave me to my work. 3B is not the only class in this school, you know."

Scarpa got up and left the room like a zombie, while the headmaster buried his head in a pile of papers, the origin and destination of which were mysteries to him. He would himself have gone home to lunch at once, but he wanted to give Scarpa time to get clear, so as not to risk running into him in the street.

Once outside the school, Scarpa didn't quite know which direction to take. He felt as if the world had come to an end. He felt as if, outside the school, nothing was real; even the road home was lost to him. Nevertheless he trod it, with such methodical steps that they seemed to have survived everything, and seemed not even his, but part of that unreal world. What would become of him now, in those empty hours with nothing to do but bounce from wall to wall, flee from voices, or study the lagging hands of his watch as they covered their course?

Luckily Marina, now that she felt herself mistress of his life, no longer took much interest in it. Over lunch they exchanged the inevitable "How are things?", "Oh, nothing new," and then didn't meet again until late that night.

Scarpa spent the afternoon and evening thinking that he must be sad, sadder than he had ever been. Undoubtedly his life, in just a few months, had gone to pieces, collapsing all around him, like a pile of plates carelessly stacked on a dresser, burying him in things he must do and things he must not do, both equally brittle and stifling. The ground was sliding away under his feet, and he had nothing left to hold on to.

Night came, and Michele pulled the sheets right over his head.

"I can see you, my little dicky-bird . . ." Marina said, spitting out the words in a menacing way as she got into bed. "Hold on, my face-cream."

She smothered herself with a strong-scented cream, and took his penis in her hand: "Don't think you can get away from me, my little dick!"

"Listen, dear, I just don't feel like it this evening. You look lovely, though," said Michele, hoping to get out of it lightly that way.

"'I feel like it, I don't feel like it!' What a load of crap, Michele! It's me that feels like it. D'you really think we can only make love when *you* feel like it? You phallocratic fart you! *I'll* make you feel like it!"

Marina began to fondle him in a mechanical manner, and as soon as his cock was hard enough, pushed it inside her and began to bounce up and down on his stomach, tossing her head about and emitting a whole gamut of moans. There was no way of ignoring this exhibition. Michele began to touch her a bit here and a bit there – breasts, buttocks, anus – and to respond with equal energy but without enthusiasm to her sounds, trying to camouflage himself with noises and

102

gestures so as to avoid being interrogated by her too. At a certain moment it seemed that things had come to a head. Marina flopped down beside him with a deep sigh, and at once asked: "Did you come, my little dicky-bird?"

"Yes, yes," Michele hastened to answer, in order to avoid a repeat, this time devoted to his pleasure.

"Funny . . . I feel pretty dry."

"You know . . . It's been a tiring day, an odd one."

"Something the matter, little dicky-bird? Tell me."

"Heavens, I wouldn't know where to start. You really want me to tell you?"

"Go ahead, tell me the lot. I like it when you talk. Makes me feel sleepy."

Marina cuddled down in his arms and half-closed her eyes. "Turn the light off . . ." Michele reached out an arm, and found himself feeling much better in the dark.

"O.K, well . . . I guess if I had to begin at the beginning, I'd have to start from the day I was born. However, you might get bored, so I'll skip a largish bit. I'll begin from when we got married. It's odd how that happened. Can you remember at all?"

"Mmmm . . . No . . . Can't remember."

"You poor dear, are you tired? I'll cut it short then. Ever since we got married I've been feeling more and more feeble – scared of everything. Sorry about all this side-tracking, but there's such a lot I want to tell you, and you and I never speak to each other, basically, even if we're talking all the time. What it comes to is that at school today . . . And here again there's a heap of things I've never talked about, like what it's like to be a teacher. Or about that creep of a headmaster . . . But maybe I'll give that a miss as well. So what happened was, he advised me to stay away, said it would be better for everyone if I went on sick-leave for these last few months of the term, and we talk it over again in October. Are you with me? Marina?" The poor thing was fast asleep.

Now that his eyes had grown accustomed to the dark, Michele could see her smooth skin, her peaceful, relaxed expression, as if she were embracing someone in a dream, as if sleep had absolved her of the rigours of living. He looked at her lips that protruded as if for a kiss, and from which every so often there grew a bubble of saliva.

"Poor thing, who knows what a rotten hard day she's had as well . . . marriage is certainly the most extraordinary thing," he thought to himself. "In all these years of casual fucking I wouldn't have bet a crooked sixpence on her, and now she's turned out to be my one consolation at this bloody awful moment. It took the bitterness of my young bachelor days to bring me so much happiness."

He went to sleep happy, and dreamt of her all through the night. Only in the very last moments before waking did the headmaster intrude into the dream. He was outside on the landing with his thumb on the bell, and wanted to know why Scarpa hadn't come to school that morning. He woke up with a start, shut off the alarm clock, without thinking, got hastily into his clothes, saying "It's late, it's late," over and over again. Marina, who seemed to be still sound asleep, murmured, "What time will you be back?"

"One o'clock. I'm teaching all morning."

He didn't want to meet the headmaster on the stairs, keeping an eye out for latecomers as was his habit. He'd have to run. He didn't make it, and had to get the caretaker to open the main door. Then he bounded up the stairs two at a time to the first floor, and rushed towards 3B.

"Scarpa!" he heard someone calling from behind. "I thought you were ill." It was the headmaster.

"Can't say I am, really," Michele answered, trying to get his breath back.

"Then you must be mad," the headmaster said with conviction and no little ill humour.

"Mad? Why?"

"Tell me, you half-wit, unless you think it is I who am the half-wit, do I speak in riddles?"

"I don't quite know . . ."

"What do you mean, you don't quite know? Imbecile! Don't you understand that you are *ill*? That I don't want to set eyes on you for the rest of the year?"

Only then did Michele remember yesterday's interview and understand why the headmaster was insulting him so liberally.

"I'm sorry, sir, I'd forgotten . . ."

"Forgotten, my foot! You were trying to put one across me. Just try to remember that I wasn't born yesterday."

"I'll leave this minute, sir. Please excuse me, sir."

The door into 3B having been left ajar, the pupils heard every word of this dialogue. They were left feeling slightly dazed, because the previous afternoon they had made up their minds to ask for their teacher's dismissal, and there was now no time to reorganize themselves. That instant the headmaster strode into the classroom, saw Robazza sitting in his usual place, and hurled himself at him in a rage. "And yet another imbecile, I see! Didn't *you* hear what I told you yesterday?"

Robazza, who had let his friends persuade him to come back to school that morning, tried to disappear into the collar of his jersey.

"Get up, you young idiot!" shouted the headmaster. And the whole class rose to its feet.

"What's this? A revolution? Shall I call the police?"

Robazza was the only one who had remained seated, and instinctively the headmaster grabbed the boy by the arm and endeavoured to wrench him from his desk.

"Let go of him at once, sir, or I shall report *you* to the police," said Nina in a firm voice. She had not the slightest idea whether any such thing were possible, but at this point there was no way of backing down.

"What will you report me for, Contin?"

"Ill treatment."

"Thank your stars you're a girl . . ."

"Let go of Robazza this minute, or you'll be in trouble."

The headmaster himself had no idea whether he could be reported, but thought it wise to let go of Robazza's arm all the same.

"Is that better now?" he found himself saying, almost as if to make sure that the report would not be made. Robazza sat down again, and the whole class did the same.

"Let's get this thing over with," the headmaster continued hastily, "before your lack of discipline creates worse problems for me. Robazza, I imagine you have understood for yourself by now – that sort of drawing is not on. This said, those drawings were done five years ago. And so if I'm now pardoning you, this should not be read as weakness on my part, but as stemming rather from the hope that these years have wrought a change in you – and for the better, I should say.

"Unfortunately, at this time when we are so close to your final exams, I have bad news for you all. Dr Scarpa is not at all well, and will not be able to finish the school year. This automatically forecloses your protest of yesterday, as I shall instruct his successor to take no notice of the marks in the register. I myself have come to realize that your teacher had a marked tendency towards pessimism. Not all ills are sent to harm us, as the old saying goes. Now you all have a chance to catch up, and go to your examinations with a better set of term marks. So buckle down to your work now and forget everything else. I shall make it my business to provide you with the peaceful surroundings you need. Now back to work. Good day."

"Excuse me, sir," asked Nina, "what has our teacher got?"

"Something serious, I fear. A nervous disease. The lungs . . . Who knows if I'll ever be able to re-employ him!"

"But wasn't he here this morning?" interrupted Ferri. "Weren't you speaking to him a moment ago in the corridor?"

"Quite right – he had come to tell me he was ill. Aren't you pleased?"

"Well, if he really does have this frightful illness . . ." began Nina, a little incredulous.

"Oh no no no no no no no!" The headmaster hastened to smooth things over. "He's not as ill as all *that*. We have advised him to take a period of rest, which should do him good. But in any case, I don't want you to worry about that. Just get down to your studies, and you will see that everything will be all right."

"What has our working hard got to do with it . . .?" Nina started to ask. But the headmaster interrupted her.

"That's enough questions. I am very touched, I must say, by the interest you show. I see your hearts are in the right place. You feel an affection for your teacher, and are worried about his health. I am proud of you. But all this is none of your business. Now just keep quiet. I must leave you alone for the rest of this hour. Good day."

On leaving the school Michele again turned towards home. "What an ass I've made of myself. It seems that the headmaster is perfectly right. I do need a holiday, if I go round forgetting what he told me only yesterday," he thought to himself, and felt slightly better. He was no longer affected by yesterday's feeling of dismay, and the whole episode, his own clumsiness, made him smile. The sweetly loving sensation he had felt as he watched Marina asleep during the night filled him with delight and made him want to talk endlessly to her, to make love, to kiss her so thoroughly as to make her even more contented than she always said she was. Wrapped in her embrace, there would be no more headmaster, no more pupils, no more café, no more nothing, only her kisses, day after day, and all those fine phrases that came flooding into his mind that maybe he would make into a book . . . But no, a book was just a commonplace concern. No, she and she alone. And rest.

He gently opened the front door, and closed it quietly behind him. The silence was complete, the shutters still all closed – what peace! She must still be asleep, he thought, and tiptoed towards the bedroom, feeling himself already in her arms, enveloped in the soft cloud of her love, so that even the few seconds which still separated them seemed full of her.

His eyes were not yet accustomed to the dark, and he felt his way forward silently so as not to wake her. He heard the sweet sounds of her sleeping. Love-sounds. She was curled up in an odd position, at the end of the bed. He passed his fingers through her hair, and she answered, already wakened and alive to love, with a slight movement of the head. The love-sounds grew louder and strangely deeper while he was wakening her with this caress; the odd thing was that they seemed to come from the region of her feet. He must certainly be suffering from exhaustion. He must rest, rest!

"Give it a good suck, you whorish sow!"

"My God," cried Michele, "there's a thief!"

"Holy Christ! Your husband!"

"Who's there? Marina, there's a thief."

"Get out, quick!"

"Marina, there's a thief, there's a thief. Marina, there's a thief. Marina, help!"

"Where's this thief, treasure? Where do you see him? Come on, show him to me."

"Bloody whore, there's a thief."

Michele had at last found the road to his tears. He was crying like a lamb and shouting, "There's a thief, fuck it. Filthy whore, where have you hidden him?"

"What about you? Weren't you meant to come back at one o'clock? Do you think I'm going to hang around waiting till my little dicky-bird feels like it? In any case, I know perfectly well how much you care about *me*. You'd love to get it up one of your little students. Tell the truth now! Go and stick it up her then. I shan't complain. We'll be quits then, and can forget about it."

"There's a thief, Marina! There's a thief."

"But you never even saw this thief! And for goodness sake stop snivelling."

Michele sat down with a thud on the bed. He wept for all the useless days that had brought him to this, and the despair of his last refuge invaded by a thief.

"Don't cry, my little dicky-bird. Come, and we'll forget about your thief together." And Marina put a hand on his penis.

"Keep your dirty hands off me, you damned whore."

"Damned whore? Have you gone out of your mind or something? Have you decided to behave like a phallocratic fart again? If you haven't understood how I'm made by now, don't try! Yours isn't the only cock I've had up me by a long chalk, and you're not going to keep me on the leash now."

"Oh shoot off your filthy mouth! It's about all it's good for."

Marina landed him a heavy clout.

"I am a lady, and expect to be treated as such. You understand?"

"You're a whore, a whore, a whore," Michele began to yell, lashing out at her. They ended up making violent love one against the other, as if to forget.

For some days, there was a mysterious, tacit understanding between them that Michele, having been wronged, was right, and in this he took a childish pleasure. It was not long, however, before Marina regained her power.

For several weeks, Michele contemplated the possibility of going back to his mother. The misery of his married life was heavy to bear. But in the end he resigned himself to it.

7

Maria had started to haggle over prices. "Mother of God, are they made of gold, these oranges?"

"It's not me that fixes the prices, Mum, I can tell you."

"Who does then?"

"The Common Market. From the time they're picked to the time they're on my barrow, there's many a one gets a bite out of 'em."

"Maybe. But why must it be me who feeds all these people?"

"You and the others, I reckon."

"I reckon you're right. Just for today, though, I think I'll give them a miss."

"Right-ho, Mum. I can let you have them for a thousand lire a dozen, *as* it's you."

"That's good of you, mister; I wouldn't have asked, of course. But I saw you were a real gentleman, and so . . ."

"Yes, yes, I'm used to your sort, Mum. The same old story every morning."

"It's not just the money, you know, I like to get the low-down, have a bit of a chat . . ."

"I know you don't mean it badly, Mum. Mind you come again, I'll always give you a good price."

Every once in a while Maria would invent a fictitious little commission for Granny, who, as soon as she had five thousand lire in her fist, immediately rang up her cronies. "Listen, dearie, I've just had a little windfall, are you busy? I'll wait for you then, at the *Due Spade*, and we'll have a little something together."

At supper-time, Nina had to go searching for her from one dive to another and, when she eventually found her, contrive to say in the most severe tone possible, "Have you gone mad, Gran?"

"Me? Yes, why? You too?"

This left Nina quite unable to utter a single one of the speeches she had been rehearsing along the way.

"Me too! Absolutely!"

"Thank goodness for that! Get yourself a chair then, and a glass, and come and sit right here."

When Nina was at last settled into the group, her grand-mother began to give a résumé of the conversation which had held her and her friends enthralled around the bottle.

"Ines here – who's known you since you were knee-high to a grasshopper – well, this summer she took a trip to the islands in the south . . . You want to tell it yourself, Ines?"

"Well, it was like this, dearie. One morning I went down to the beach, see, to get a bit of sunbathing, and while I'm lying there, up comes this gent in his boat, see? Young, handsome, all got up posh. He must have been twenty years younger than me – at least. 'Doing a bit of sunbathing, Miss?' he says to me. And me, I says, 'Yes, and what's it to you?'

"'S'pose you wouldn't like to buy a fish?' And he pulls out somethin' smellin' to high heaven!"

"Get on with it, woman," Gran interrupted. "This smelly part of the story seems a bit fishy to me. Anyway, fish or no fish, the fellow's written her a lovely long letter: 'Dear Lady . . .'"

"'Beautiful Lady,'" Ines corrected, laying much stress on the e-sound.

"'Beautiful Lady,'" Gran repeated, "'I have thought of you so much, that if it's convenient, I'd like to pay a call on you in Venice.' Then all kinds of bowings and scrapings, you know, like the way they go on in the south."

"He's from the Lipari Islands," another one chirped in with a knowing air, "down there near Sardinia."

"Sicily, you goose."

"Doesn't matter which, Sardinia or Sicily, they're both dumps!"

"You're just ignorant. Have a drink and shut up," Gran cautioned her, refilling her glass. Then, turning to Nina: "What do you say, pet, shall we get him up here?"

"It could be dangerous, you know," the ignorant one put in.

"Oh, no, no, not at all," Ines objected, "nothing to be afraid of with that one. He was very proper."

"Pipe down, and let Nina get a word in edgeways, bless us. Let's hear what the young folk have to say."

"Will he pay for his own ticket?" Nina asked.

"Naturally, my dear."

"Then what have you got to lose, Ines?"

"That's right! Let him come. And if roses bloom, so much the better. If not, we'll have a good laugh about it," Nina's grandmother said, bringing the conversation to an end.

Then she took Nina's hand. "Come on, pet, your eyes are only half open. Let's get along home, and don't you worry your head about anything."

They set off towards home, and every so often Gran said, "Bless you, child, go a bit slower. I've plenty of heart left, but I've not too much in the legs."

She wanted to hear about Luca. Things she had already been told a hundred times, like when he had kissed her and fallen on his face. And stopping to get her breath back she would say, "That's lovely for you, Nina. What a lovely boy you've found yourself."

Nina could find nothing to say to this, and hurried on.

Meanwhile, Luca had got into the habit of going every evening after supper to listen to music with Marco, or to talk about the books which were willingly lent him by his new friend. Marco had seen where he could second Luca's interest along certain lines, which talents were worth encouraging and which naïveties needed correcting. He had in fact become his teacher. Luca tried to learn as much as he could, for everything Marco said seemed so well put and so right that in the end he was unable to make any objections. From Marco came the vocabulary he found himself using, the accent, the turns of phrase, even the slight slouch he affected in his walk. And the more Luca tried to escape from this plagiarism, the more apparent were the signs of his dependence, so that in the end, the only way he could draw a line between himself and his teacher was to keep silent. Instead of accepting the fact that he was fond of his friend, and had learnt a very great deal from him, Luca decided to go back out of their friendship and somehow try to cancel it.

In the end he made up his mind to break with Marco; and not only with him, but with everything that had sprung up from their friendship. He hid himself in fashions and ambiguities, and in the obscure rhetoric of easy answers. He had become a Caliban, ready to be the slave of a drunken store-keeper simply so as to be able to rebel, and he was forced to serve the most fierce and pitiless of masters: his own rancour. He reacted against Marco, and against that physical and intellectual decadence which in the end aided and abetted his rebellious frame of mind. Nonetheless, it was precisely in his confused attempt to escape that the sense of poetry began to take shape in Luca. He felt something inside himself begin to stir, to reflect form, human beings, or the movement of water. And in this reflection was a space for his feelings, which were anyway far too detached from what was actually happening.

The days followed their usual empty routine of school, meals, sleep, study. Luca wished he could disappear from this life, and let himself be drawn into the secret world he felt in his heart, and which he thought could exist only in the derangement of the senses, in the anarchy of habits. He cried out continually to his muse, "Where are you hiding, damn you!" Every day he noticed less of what was going on around him, and sank ever deeper into a pit of despondency.

Nina followed this metamorphosis with a certain detachment, but it frightened her. Once in a while Luca came to her house to study and prepare for oral tests, but was quite unable to concentrate. He knew even the longest poems by heart, usually without understanding what he was reciting; he was sensually infatuated by the rhythm, the colour of the language, but the meaning of the thing eluded him. His very way of thinking became daily less adapted to school-work, and Nina, who knew what was in store for them both, tried to redivert his attention and force him to learn a handful of formulae, which she hoped would save his face with the examiners.

"You're so pedantic, Nina, you're always dragging me back to the obvious. Try to follow what I'm saying, instead of checking to see if it's there in the anthology."

"Do you think I'm enjoying it? If you answer like that in the exam, if you go on about delirium and the derangement of the senses, all they're going to say is, 'Now listen here, if anyone is deranged around here it's you,' and simply send you home."

"So let them. I'm trying to understand how we work, what it really means to read, to live . . ."

"Couldn't you possibly wait until after the exams?"

"What the hell are you saying? This is life, you know; there's no way you can just put it off."

"I know."

"No you don't, you don't understand a thing. You agree with me as if I were a madman, but out of the corner of your eye you're looking to see what page we've got to, and thinking what a lot of time we're wasting, admit it! I'm better off by myself. I'll see you at school. 'Bye."

What the real motive for his rage was, Luca could not tell. He found the answer to a thousand questions a day, but the answers came too easily. It no longer cost him either courage or honesty to observe the conventionalities of the world. It was as if he were ricocheted from one superficiality to another, repeating the same banalities in reverse.

Meanwhile, as he wandered around Venice, even the lamp-posts seemed sad. He felt that something irretrievable had happened between himself and the world, that he would never be able to return to his old self, because behind everything he now found something else, behind every meaning another meaning. He was lost in a hall of mirrors with no beginning and no end. He examined his future with a jaundiced, deprecating eye. Every kind of career was abhorrent to him – he would not be a musician nor anything else. He no longer allowed anyone to come near him, would not have his hair cut, answered gruffly even if someone asked "Would you like some coffee?" He wanted to sever his ties with everyone. Out with Marco, out with his parents, Nina, the whole lot of them!

Nina didn't want to lose him, and always found some justification or other for his rudeness. At bottom, Nina told herself, nothing had changed between them. Luca was becoming a savage beast, but beneath the nervous, irritable words which he used to keep her at a distance, she could still see the boy who had fallen from the sky for a kiss and then run away like a thief who has just stolen a treasure. They were still joined, like a mollusc to its shell, like a man to his skin.

Then one day Luca telephoned. "Nina, I want to see you. I'll wait for you at the Zattere."

"O.K, I'll be there in half an hour." Nina closed her philosophy textbook thinking, "Right, page 115, I'll be seeing you shortly."

Luca was sitting at a table outside a bar, gazing out over the Giudecca, at the boats, the seagulls, the choppy water of the channel. Nina came up to him slowly, thinking of page 115 and of how cold it was outside. She felt strangely uncomfortable now that she was only a few steps away from him. Luca sneezed, and searched in his pocket for a handkerchief; Nina turned round and walked hurriedly in the direction of home, thinking, "If he sees me now and runs after me, what shall I say?" But Luca didn't run after her, and after a hundred yards or so Nina again stopped and turned round, and began to walk falteringly in his direction. Luca was still gazing over the canal, with that vague, lost expression which would never get him through his exams. Nina didn't go nearer, she just watched him and felt sorry for him, as she tried to summon up the kind of bright, clear voice that would say "Hi, Luca," like a herald's trumpet, and cure him of all his dejection. But she was afraid that if she opened her mouth, instead of pure clarion tones, she would give voice to her embarrassment in half-formed, uncertain phrases.

She went home, reopened her philosophy textbook, and let her eyes run over page 115. But her thoughts were elsewhere, imagining Luca's hurt like a vulture perched on top of the wardrobe, waiting to swoop on whoever would be the first to weaken. Her eyes ran over the page, backwards and forwards, page 115, begging her mind not to think about this and that but to concentrate on what the book was saying. After some minutes, maybe a few, maybe many, the doorbell rang and it was Luca.

"Why didn't you come?"

"I've got to work, Luca."

"Look, you can work later. Come on, I've got something important to say to you."

Nina took her coat and went down the stairs in front of him. Each step brought with it a more lugubrious thought, as if she were going down stairs into a dark, uninviting cellar. She should say something cheerful to soften him. But when she turned round to him with a smile, nothing came out but a stupid, clumsy question about school, and a desperate urge to cry. So she tried to take his arm, but he brushed her off with a cold gesture, to which, unfortunately, she had lately become accustomed.

"I've been treating you badly for ages. I don't know what's come over me or what to do about it. I want to be alone, Nina. We've got to split up."

There was a deathly hush on the canalside now. Where had everybody gone? And who could it have been who had spoken? Her mind rushed on ahead towards some place where she could not hear him, but his words pursued her even there, and cascaded into her mind like the rocks of a landslide. She managed to keep calm by looking straight ahead of her, by visualizing the day when they would remember this evening with a smile; and what was going to happen, and what was really happening, and it was only a matter of seconds before she would begin to scream, unless something did happen . . . "He will say something different now, for sure. Or else all these houses will crumble, and the tide will rise and drown us all."

Not the slightest sound to turn one's ear to. Nothing to wash away those words.

"Did you hear me?" Luca asked brusquely, looking into her eyes and wondering how he ever could have loved someone so ugly, so predictable and lacking in feeling.

"You don't love me any more?" Nina asked, brushing back a stray lock of his hair behind his ear. "You don't love me any more? That's the only thing I want to know . . ."

Luca looked away, for when his eyes pierced the depths of Nina's he saw again what a great and wonderful galaxy there was in that person. The tranquillity of life with her, those kisses, those caresses; and knowing where the sun would rise and where it would come to rest. He touched her face, and Nina tried to squeeze his hand between her cheek and shoulder. To Luca that face suddenly seemed like a great weight; he felt he must at all costs pull free of its orbit. He tugged his hand away and thrust it into his pocket.

"Let's just leave it at that, Nina, it's better."

He turned as if, instead of leaving Nina, he had just thrown away half a ham roll, and walked quickly away. Nina saw him climb the wooden steps of the bridge two at a time, and disappear down the other side as if swallowed up by a fold of darkness. The sound of his footsteps faded and silence returned, like the silence of a theatre after a standing ovation, when the tenor has left the stage; there is nothing left but for Nina to say "Away away!"

Snow was falling tonight and its too perfect quietness left Nina alone with Luca's words, which she had not yet really taken in. Was it *possible* he had just gone off like that? "No, it can't be, he'll ring and we'll make it up. We didn't even quarrel! And even if he does want to be by himself, we don't necessarily have to break up. He could have said 'I don't love you any more,' or even just 'No . . .' My question was straightforward enough. O.K, he never really understood a straightforward question . . . How quiet it is! There might at least be someone yelling tonight. Not a soul, damn it, quiet as mice. If only someone would cry out, I could say to myself: look, Nina, there's someone in despair, poor thing! Even the noise of a washing-machine and I could say: listen, Nina, how sad it is! Not a sound, no one to help me. I wonder where Luca's gone? Not that I'm thinking of going to look for him. In fact it's him who ought to come and look for me. What have I done wrong? How cold this silence is. I'll cry out then, so that if, maybe, there's another Nina out there, she'll say: 'Listen to that poor Nina. Tonight she's in despair.'"

The more her thoughts, one by one, were being gathered into the arms of sadness, like a shepherd gathering his sheep into the fold, the more they attempted to relish those last moments of uncertainty, engage themselves in senseless questions, in yes–no, no–yes without any context, in a strange, idiotic euphoria.

It began to snow heavily, and Nina started running across Campo Santa Margherita thinking, "Better off without that madman," abandoning herself to that feast of softness and whiteness. She tried to call to mind all that was most beautiful for her in this world – fresh clean sheets; her father calling her with outstretched arms and tossing her in the air, her father hiding his face behind a napkin, then reappearing, laughing. And every time he hides his face Nina thinks he has gone, that they have left her, left her alone in the world. What misery! It is a cruel game, but a useful and necessary one, because one learns that when a face disappears it is not for always. He's behind the napkin, I know he is. I'm not afraid; now he'll pop out. There he is!

"There he is!"

Nina looked at each corner of the square in turn, alert, gay, optimistic . . . It's not easy, but I'm happy, and lucky

– now I'll shut my eyes and count to five, and Luca will reappear. Then we'll be with one another this beautiful snowy night, and sleep together at Marco's. I know you're only just round the corner, damn it. Come back. That's enough. Come back.

"Come back, my love, come back."

But Luca did not reappear. Nina's feet were wet, and she thought she had better run home before she caught her death. She got into bed at once and started to stare in a dazed way at a point in the darkness, waiting for sleep. "If I manage to get to sleep, it won't dare to swoop on me," she thought, eyeing the vulture perched on top of the wardrobe at the end of her bed. A moment later the sky was light and it was day. Nina got up as if in a bad dream, washed, and went to school.

Luca had wandered about the whole night, trying to shake off his own footsteps and his own thoughts. The sun rose behind him, then came the first early risers. The gulls were flying low. It wasn't snowing any more, but everything was wet. He saw a person hurrying along the other bank to catch the ferry. The next one will be crowded.

It's day. Soon there will be no more peace. Must run home before I'm caught, must get to school. More light, more people. The stones become luminous. Then the sun. A door opening behind him, very close, and someone staring at him. The person's eyes like a wound in his back. More and more people. The children all crowding round the doorway. School. Nina's there too, beautiful as a flower.

He passed the morning without uttering a word. Then he found himself at home, and his mother talking, his father talking. School. Of course, they were talking about school.

"Nothing. Nothing's happened."

Water. What is water like? Like a mass of demi-semiquavers, as quick as the reflections of light – how stupid not to have thought of it before. And the oar, it's obvious, the oar in two-four time. The gondola, now, that has no time signature, just one long, unvarying sound. At least at the beginning it's like that, then it divides as well – in two? In two-four or in four-four. All these sounds are deep. Even the movement of the water (which has reflections in the higher register) is in fact a low sound, fathomless. The chords expand – the scream of the gulls, the whistle of a steamer – all simple chords, but growing ever richer. And a woman's voice, racked with despair, alone, forsaken, weeping. A legato melodic line which at times repeats an older, deeper theme: solitude. Yes, exactly, and she embraces a sorrow greater than herself, an infinity of notes, that can scarcely fit into the compass of the voice.

"Luca, aren't you eating?" his mother asked him.

"No, I'm not hungry. I'm sorry." Luca disappeared at once to his room, while his parents both remained open-mouthed at that "sorry". It was a word which had seemed to have vanished for ever from Luca's vocabulary.

At the piano, pen in hand, he tried to write down the idea that was dangling before his eyes like a carrot in front of a donkey. He worked for two hours, then called his sister Silvia.

"Silvia, can you read this music?"

"It's unsingable, Luca. The notes are too long."

"Of course, and it's written for a contralto too, not for a squeaky little soprano like you. But let's try it all the same."

Luca began to play the accompaniment for his sister, but Silvia stopped every few notes to take a breath.

"No, Silvia. You must manage at least this one legato, otherwise we're not together. Try breathing *here*. Take a deep breath and hold these three bars. I'll speed up a bit to help you, but don't let the voice give out. Let's try again."

Little by little Luca began to hear the piece. He retouched

a few notes, added a pause here and there, and became increasingly pleased and excited. Silvia's voice was far too light; a fuller, more sensual voice was needed, but if possible, equally youthful. While the music moulded and adjusted itself, almost on its own, it seemed, he could at last allow himself the feelings which, in order to compose, he had had to lay aside; he could understand the emotions he had attempted to depict, so that even Silvia's treble voice gave him pleasure. What peace, what freedom, what relief! So this awful day of torment, cold, cruelty, was over.

"Well done, Nina, you sing it really well. It's there, it's there, I've written it! Do you like it? Tell me."

Silvia had begun to giggle.

"What's up, don't you like it? Tell me right now what's the matter. You don't like it, is that it?"

"No, it's good, Luca, I like it."

"Have I made mistakes in the harmony?"

"Oh no, no, of course not. I'm laughing because you didn't even notice you called me Nina. You love her so much that we all seem to have become Ninas."

Luca looked on coldly at Silvia's giggles.

"Go away now, please," he said to her. "I want to be alone."

"You're not offended, are you? Come on, let's try it again."

"GET OUT!" he yelled, and as soon as the terrified Silvia was through the door, he locked himself in. Luca's mother and father hastened to Silvia who was snivelling in the passage.

"He's mad, completely mad!"

Banging his fist peremptorily on the door, his father shouted: "Come out of there at once!"

"Why?" asked Luca from inside.

"To beg your sister's pardon."

"Sorry, Silvia."

"Not like *that*. I told you to come out. What are you doing, locked in there? Taking drugs? Open the door at once."

"Please give me five minutes."

Now that Luca had recognized Nina in his contralto with a voice as warm as tears, a shadow had fallen over the music. Had he had to make such a mess of everything then, just to write a few paltry notes? So this was what his muse was: a vampire? Now that it had sunk its fangs into its victims, he saw it all clearly. What should he do now? How would he be able to love, knowing he was making such a use of his life, and of the lives of others? And it was not just a question of loving. There was laughter, looking, weeping, playing, hoping, too. Why, then, accept these conditions? Why not impose others? Who says that this is Nina? "My heart says it."

In a nearby courtyard children were playing ball, calling and answering each other by name. The happiness in which life serves only itself, on the other side of the window panes of those few notes just written, was finished and far away. In the broad sky that covered the city with blue he saw Nina's white throat, her flowing hair, the kisses abandoned the night before, all ready to be turned to music. Nothing as yet surpassed her in his heart, no idea, no other woman. But how far away she seemed. And how his love for her had changed. His feeling for her was stronger than ever, yet he didn't reach for the telephone; it didn't enter his head to seek her out . . . "You love that girl so much that we've all become Ninas." True. The sky is Nina, I am Nina. We are all the tears of a forsaken woman.

"Luca!" his father shouted again. Luca opened the door and his mother immediately put a hand to his forehead and said with alarm, "The boy has a fever!"

At which his father felt excused from admonishing and questioning his son, and with a gruff "Very well" left the room.

It passed through Luca's mind that it was already time to leave that house, that he had no right to ruin the lives of such gentle people. But he let himself be put to bed with a cup of tea.

Next day Nina telephoned, and Signora Brandi told her that Luca was in bed with a temperature and couldn't come to the telephone. Was there any message? "No, nothing, thank you. It was just a little thing. But if he's ill it doesn't matter."

So he was ill, she couldn't see him. If only she could meet him at school, run into him somewhere, say hello. But he was not there, didn't telephone, maybe no longer existed. She confided in no one. In the evening, after clearing the table, and when she felt sadness creeping over her, Nina went to her room to study page 115 of her philosophy textbook, because thinking brought a lump into her throat and her thoughts turned to tears in her eyes. In the darkness and silence all around her bed, she would search for any image at all of Luca; would try to remember some phrase or some episode which might explain what was happening now. Some lie, even, with which in a flight of fantasy she could oppose the sorry certainty of this loneliness.

8

"Quick, Nina, get some clothes on and run and fetch the doctor. Hurry up, for heaven's sake. Your Gran's bad."

Nina opened her eyes. Her mother, distraught and dishevelled, was shaking her out of sleep. She threw on her clothes. It was four in the morning.

"Run, I've already telephoned, and he says he won't come at this hour of the morning. Go and lean on the doorbell until you get him out of bed." A sound of heavy, laboured breathing pervaded the house, like liquid flowing from a vessel and slowly, inexorably spreading. Nina glimpsed her father's back in her grandmother's room, rushed on down the stairs, ran to the house on the corner of the canalside, pressed her thumb on the doctor's doorbell and kept it there.

"Do you want to kill me off too?" snapped the doctor, opening the door after nearly ten minutes. "Let's hope it's something serious, dear Miss Contin: calling me out at this hour doesn't come cheap, I can tell you. And I told your mother so too."

"Please hurry, doctor, and we'll sort out the money later."

"All right then, let's go."

The room was in darkness. As soon as he entered, the doctor turned on the bedside light, and Nina saw her grandmother's face; it was flushed and contorted with effort. A stertorous breathing came from her constricted throat, with terrifying slowness. It was horrible to hear, like the creaking of oars or the rusty, dislocated hinges of an ancient door.

After a short examination the doctor led Maria out of the room by her arm.

"It's pulmonary oedema. Call the priest if you want, but in my opinion there's not even time for that. Give me fifty thousand lire, Signora Contin, and I'll go back to bed."

Maria went to her bedroom and came out with her purse in her hand, pulled out a note and gave it to the doctor; she followed him to the front door, waiting for him to tell her what they should do next. But the doctor opened the door and went down the stairs without another word.

Nina was watching her father, whose attention was riveted to those heaving gasps. That noise like rasping iron, the darkness, the bedside lamp, the flushed face, the physical pain, were all mirrored in his body. Seated on a stool by the bed, he seemed hypnotized by the sound of that breathing. He followed it each time as it died away, and each time as it tautened again like a swelling sail. To Nina that fixed, unemotional interest was scary; she would have liked to say "Come away, Dad," but for a long time now there had not been the kind of understanding between herself and her father that would allow her to say such a thing – an order is sometimes an intimate thing, when it recognizes the authority of affection.

Maria stood leaning against the doorway, trying to think of something she could do to help. And it distracted her for a moment or two to feel there might be something she could do. Then she put her hands over her face and wept quietly, smothering her sobs as if they were something no one should know about. Again she felt she must make some move, and drying her eyes, looked impatiently at Nina. Then she turned back to her mother and covering her face, let the quiet tears come.

Gran breathed on, slowly and exhaustedly, until dawn; suddenly, she fixed her eyes on Nina, and her mouth started to open and shut, mouthing something.

"What does she want, Nina? Does she want a drink – what's she saying?" Maria begged. Nina, in an effort to understand what her grandmother wanted, tried to copy the movement of her lips, and found herself mouthing a kiss. She took Gran's hand and began to murmur in her ear:

"We were just near here. You know, behind Santa Margherita . . ." Gran closed her eyes contentedly, and Nina went on: "Luca was drunk as a lord and said to me – he couldn't stop laughing – 'Your eyes are made of flowers and I can see so many lovely stars, all inside my head, that it seems like the sky.' Then he bent down to me, like a prince, and kissed me gently, gently, and I saw all those lovely stars as well. And he kissed me again, and then again, and those soft kisses, light as feathers, smooth as running water, seemed to be star-rain, raining from his stars down, down and on to the earth."

Nina had forgotten the pain of remembering that kiss, and wanted to rid those few minutes of their weight, to make them airy and distracting for her grandmother. Gran, when she noticed the story had come to an end, twinkled an amused, mad eye at her, vulgar yet innocent, and Nina loved her, as if all the days she had loved her, all the evenings she had fished her out of the bar half drunk and taken her home on her arm, were gathered into that one moment.

The first light of day came sneaking through the window. Nina's grandmother turned her eyes to it as if someone had entered the room, or something strange had happened, "But it's only the day." The struggle to breathe was over, and she could no longer hear the gentle voices of those three last sentinels keeping vigil as she passed over the threshold, nor hear their discreetly muffled sobs, their restrained movements. "The day," she thought, "it's only the day." She looked at the clear sky beyond the window, at two clouds driven by the brisk spring breeze. She closed her eyes and drifted away with them.

"Is she sleeping?" Maria asked in alarm. Nina put her ear close to her grandmother's nostrils, kissed her, and went to hug her mother. Pietro held his wife's arm tightly for a moment as he left the room, then went and lay down on his bed. Maria finally went over to her mother, sat down by the bed and took her hand.

"Poor, dear mother, how much you've had to suffer tonight."

She stroked the dead woman's forehead and began her muffled sobbing again, full of shame for things left unsaid, for unfinished phrases, opportunities for ever lost, and then those thieving clouds.

Pietro listened for a whole hour to Maria's sobs, lying on the bed, his eyes fixed on the ceiling. It was as if, instead of alleviating grief, those short, half-smothered sobs prolonged it, kept it going, as if Maria's grief was part of her mother and keeping it alive had to do with her somehow. It was almost an entreaty, a supplication. But to Pietro these sobs merely seemed strange, and when, every so often, one of them jolted him out of his exhaustion, he wondered: "Who is that crying? It's Maria, who is my wife . . . It's my wife, who is Maria." He repeated this to himself over and over again, and as if coming back to his senses after each repetition, he then asked himself, "But why?"

He rose, shaved, retied his tie and went to work. Sitting down at his little desk in the office, surrounded by the white, silent walls that framed him now forever, he began once again to sign, stamp and certify, to certify, sign and stamp the documents which originated in an orderly pile on his left, and to stack them neatly in a twin pile on his right.

Pietro's life was a gigantic, uninterrupted rolling motion, like a boulder gathering speed on its downhill journey. He had hidden himself in a niche within this moving body, and tried not to alter its motion in the slightest way: work, Nina, Maria, talking and not talking, sleeping, eating, his pills, formed the outlines of this body, the points of contact with other moving bodies. No one prevented his steady rolling motion; and no one, to all intents and purposes, really noticed his existence any more.

Two young secretaries were giggling together in the same office, talking of their love affairs, of the Easter holidays to come. They chatted under their breath, so as not to be heard, and only an occasional "You don't say" or a peal of laughter burst out, like a bird which has revealed its hideout by moving a twig in the bushes, and takes wing – with a softly whispered "Ssh . . . listen" as a call to secrecy – to find a new refuge in the wood.

"Shall we open the window, Signor Contin? It's not cold today," asked one of them.

"Yes, yes, open it if you like. I don't mind."

It was a beautiful spring morning. The wind gave the dusty files the scent of the sea, and threatened wild confusion among the piles of papers on the desks. All of a sudden, Pietro thought he heard his mother-in-law's laboured breathing – hers or someone else's. He raised his eyes anxiously from his papers and looked around, but all was quiet: the girls giggling at their table; no one waiting for attention at the counter; just the wind barely rustling the edges of his two piles of papers.

"Did you hear anything?" he asked the girls uneasily.

"What's that, Signor Contin?"

"Didn't you hear a wheezing sound? Someone must be ill! Quick, maybe it's downstairs . . ."

The two girls exchanged glances and pulled faces at each

other. Without moving to get up, one said, "I didn't hear a thing."

"You must have heard it!"

Pietro got up and went to the window. The wheezing seemed even nearer, but down in the street all was quiet, no one was dying. The wind was moving one of the old wooden shutters, making the hinges creak. Pietro made the shutter fast with a wooden wedge and stood for a moment listening. Had the breathing really stopped?

"It's all right. It was only that old shutter. Sorry, girls, but at my age you're never sure what you're hearing and what you're not."

The two girls grinned, and he looked at them in surprise, thinking, "What are they laughing at? Poor girls, there's nothing to laugh about."

But he too smiled, so as not to embarrass them, and so they wouldn't see where he had hidden his thoughts.

The day's work drew to a close at last, and he went out into the street and began to make his way home. On the gondola crossing, he thought he heard that wheezing sound again, and he looked around carefully at the faces of the other passengers. But no, they all looked fine; no one was dying. Then, almost of its own accord, his gaze fell on the rowlocks. It was the gondolier grinding out those gasps, one by one, with the wood of his moving oar. He kept his eyes and ears fixed on that spot, hoping he had found the source of his macabre fantasy. He felt weak and a little frightened. Getting out of the gondola he slipped on a slimy step, and ended up with one foot in the water; had it not been for the prompt assistance of the gondolier, he would have fallen into the canal.

"Thank you, thanks ever so. Mother of God, my foot's soaked. But thanks again, gondolier. I'm so ancient I don't even know where I'm putting my feet these days."

The gondolier grinned, and Pietro thought once again, "There's nothing to laugh at." But he gave the gondolier a smile as well, so as to hide his thoughts.

He walked on very slowly. At San Silvestro he stopped a moment deciding which way he would take to get home. The city seemed suddenly foreign to him – the corners, the houses, the alleys. Even the short distance from office to home, which he'd walked so many times before, all those places of his habit were changed round, unrecognizable, filled with mystery. "Which way do I go now? How do I get home from here? Where was it again?" He turned left and left again, following the walls that sometimes took him to the edge of a canal, and sometimes into a courtyard; but never home. After three-quarters of an hour he was back in Campo San Silvestro. He sat himself down on the steps of the church. It was growing dark, and he wanted his supper.

"Oh Venice, Venice, even you are betraying me today."

He had been sitting on the steps for quite some time when he saw Luca loping swiftly across the square.

"Luca!" he called out. "Luca, do me a kindness and take me home. I can't find the way."

Luca led Pietro home in silence. When they came to the steps he said, "Are you O.K. now, Signor Contin?"

"I am, and many thanks. You're a good lad. Don't you want to come up and say hello to Nina?"

"No thanks, I must get home for supper."

"Why? What's the time?"

"It must be about half-past eight."

"Oh, come along in, come and cheer her up a bit. Granny died last night and we're all down in the dumps." And with a slightly over-familiar gesture he pushed Luca up the steps in front of him. Luca felt it was scarcely the moment to have a reunion with Nina, but by then Signor Contin had opened the door.

"Nina, come and see who I've brought with me," he called, happy to be home at last.

"Hush, for heaven's sake pipe down," Nina said, coming to meet them in the passage. "Mum's dropped off at last."

"Who's there?" they heard Maria's voice calling from the bedroom.

"It's me, it's me. Keep calm now," said Pietro, moving towards the bedroom.

Luca was still hovering on the doorstep. His one desire was to flee, but there wasn't time, for as soon as she saw him Nina forgot everything, all the hurt, and melted into his arms in a flood of scalding tears. He stroked her hair, an arm around her delicate shoulders, and she seemed to him then the most frail and precious creature on earth. He was glad to have found her again, even against his will, glad that he'd met her father in the street, and yielded to his request, instead of slipping away as he had wanted to, for all this had brought him back into her arms. He wanted to say, "It's all over, Nina. I'll never leave you alone again, never." And he wanted to cry with her over the thoughtless levity with which he had let her drop out of the garden of their love, leaving her in an empty, silent alley.

His eyes were dry, however. And the more he pondered on ending their separation, the more such promises – his "never again" – seemed insubstantial and superficial, like a shiny lacquer over the heart, which catches the light for an instant but which is scratched off by the first kiss, the first question, the first frank look, revealing everything that had been deliberately hidden there.

He longed for Nina's forgiveness and her love, but already, in her soft, sweet-smelling hair, through which his fingers ran as though through some miraculous spring of water – he was drawing forth notes, timbres, rhythms . . . even in the tears he sought in his own eyes, he was laying an ambush for his own emotions. "So better not to cry," he thought.

"Come in," said Nina, taking his hand. "I'll show you Gran."

The corpse was dressed in light colours and the face had a naked and ageless expression, like that of someone in a photograph, taken by surprise. The blood had coagulated at the nape of the neck, leaving the face pale – pale as the little lamp that lit the room.

"See how beautiful she is, my little Gran. You're not scared, are you, Luca? Come over here near her."

Luca came nearer and looked into Nina's eyes: they had wept all they could weep, and were ringed with angry red.

"She wanted me to tell her over again the story of our first kiss. She's so fond of that story."

Nina stroked her grandmother's hair, and Luca felt uncomfortably out of place. "They're all mad, even Nina. Doesn't she realize she's dead? Why does she talk about her as if she were alive, and smooth her hair? And that other old duffer losing his way like that – he's more Venetian than I am! I'd better get home to supper. Anyway, it's all over with Nina."

He sidled out of the room without making a sound, and vanished.

Meanwhile, Pietro had laid himself down beside Maria, stroking her cheek and smiling at her without speaking. They were just an old couple now, lying on the bed which had harboured them for so many nights. Just as in the old days, their fears were no longer locked in their individual hearts, but lost themselves in that wide bed, in their breathing, in the other person who was the whole world, who was kind, who understood. Pietro watched over Maria in her half-sleep, ready to comfort her when she was roused by some bad dream, some slight noise. Ready to snatch her away from the fears, the feelings of guilt and the torment of her regret for things left unsaid, which waited for her on the threshold of sleep. Still in their clothes, they lay there for a long while after Luca had left and Nina had gone to bed, and the night had no more noise to hide within its darkness.

"Let's get under the covers, Pietro, I'm cold."

"You're right, let's get undressed. I'm old, Maria – do you know, I got lost today."

"Wherever was that, Pietro?"

"At San Silvestro. I went round and round like an idiot for hours and landed up in the same place again. I'd forgotten the way home!"

"My poor old Pietro!"

"Then luckily I saw Luca and asked him to bring me back, because I couldn't manage alone."

"Is Luca here?"

"Calm down, now. He'll have left ages ago."

"Why, whatever time is it?"

"It's a quarter to three."

"Goodness me, have I slept all that time?"

"You slept a bit."

"Did you offer Luca a drink? He comes from a good classy family, you know."

"I didn't offer him anything. I left him with Nina and she had a good cry with him, which'll do them more good than anything."

"Poor little thing! She loved her granny a lot, that one."

"It can't be helped. It happens to all of us . . . Tell me, Mum, you feeling any better yourself now?"

"I feel a bit tired still. And I'm still fuming about that pig of a doctor. I'd like to run after him and get my fifty thousand lire back, and teach him a few manners, and a bit of respect for other people's deaths."

"What's the point of that? Take it easy now."

"Pietro, if I die, promise you'll call a different doctor?"

"I promise, Maria."

"Right. Let's get some sleep then – tomorrow's going to be another hard day. Goodnight, Dad."

"Goodnight, Maria."

"D'you want me to take you to the office tomorrow?"

"No, you'll have too much to do."

"You know what we'll do? You leave the house when Nina starts for school, and go along with her."

"I wouldn't want her to notice anything . . ."

"Don't you worry about that. I'll tell her I'm worried about you being all topsy-turvy after Granny dying, and get her to go with you."

"No, forget it. Her school's at San Trovaso isn't it?"

"You'll just have to leave a bit early, the pair of you. Let's get a wink of sleep, Pietro."

Pietro slept little. Sometimes he fell into a half sleep, but never a deep one. He heard his mother-in-law's death-rattle in everything now; in creaking wood, in a boat sliding over the lagoon, in the wind whispering among the chimney-pots. Only when his eye fell on the little woman sleeping at his side did his fear abate.

In the morning they all three rose early, and had their breakfast. Then Maria, having given Nina her instructions, buttoned up her husband's coat collar. Pietro stared at her for a moment, lost, allowing her to straighten his tie, adjust his coat, without a word. Then he fixed his bright, furtive eyes on the corner of the ceiling to hide the fear in them and the impossible child-like prayer he wanted to address to her and the world – never to have to go out to work again, never to be plucked out of that embrace which was his only haven.

Maria straightened Pietro's tie yet again, avoiding his

glance, but all the while she sensed his anguish at leaving the house that morning, and she burst into tears, clutching the lapels of the coat in which he stood bundled, ready to be dragged into a world which laughed at his stumbling steps, laughed at phantom death-rattles, at his soaking foot, at the love caught unawares which led him to search the street continuously for someone dying there. Little did he notice that it was he himself who was gradually dying, day by day.

Nina ascribed her mother's tears to Granny's death, but was shocked to see them flowing like that in front of her father.

She set off at a good pace; Pietro followed a few yards behind, keeping a close eye on their path and trying to memorize at least one or two landmarks. At the door of the office building Nina kissed him on both cheeks.

"Bye-bye, Dad. Do you want me to come and fetch you at two o'clock?"

"I'd really like that, if you can manage it."

"O.K, see you at two."

Pietro watched her as she hurried off at a quick step, to be in time for school.

"How like Maria she is," he thought, "with her little short legs, and her funny brisk walk."

But as soon as he crossed the threshold of the Town Hall he found he was lost again. He began to traipse slowly and timidly through the great rooms and corridors looking for his office, until someone eventually stopped him.

"What are you doing wandering around like a poor mutt, Contin?"

"Me? I was looking for the boss. Do you know where he is?"

"In his office, I imagine."

"Would you mind showing me the way?"

"What? You don't know the way, after all these years?"

"I seem to have forgotten it."

The other man laughed. And Pietro defended himself with the faintest of smiles, as he desperately tried to remember his colleague's name. He followed him, marvelling at how he turned to left or to right without apparent difficulty.

"Gaspareto!" Pietro exclaimed cheerfully.

"What's the matter?"

"Aren't you Gaspareto?"

"So what?"

"Nothing, nothing, I'm just glad. Thanks so much for your help."

Gaspareto started to laugh and completely dispelled the pleasure Pietro had felt at remembering the name. That laughter brought home to him the frightfulness of his confusion which seemed so comic to everyone else, but in which he saw a fearful threat: the threat of not being in a condition to work, support himself, Nina and Maria and keep the horde of landlords and taxmen at bay. Until now he had managed it – he'd kept them out of his house. He was the only breadwinner in the family, and without his earnings there was nothing but the intolerable brutality of poverty, with which both he and Maria were all too well acquainted.

They made him wait a few minutes outside the boss's door while Gaspareto went in to announce him, and as he stood there he heard another of those ghastly laughs. Then he was shown in.

"Sit down, Contin. What can I do for you?"

"Excuse me, sir, but I don't think I am any longer in a fit condition to come to work. I keep forgetting everything, I don't know what to do . . ."

The boss asked a secretary to bring him the folder containing Pietro's records of employment at the Town Hall; it was all there, listed and classified.

"You have only eight months to go until you receive your pension, Contin, did you know that?" he said at last, very solemnly.

"No, I don't know anything about it."

"You started work here at a late age by our standards, you know. Of course, there was the war. And you had to get your diploma as best you could by going to night classes. You did very well. But the minimum here is fifteen years, through no fault of mine, I might add. You hang on for eight months, which, if you haven't yet had your holiday, become seven. More than that I can't do for you."

"Excuse me, sir, but it's not from lack of wanting to – not laziness. It's just that I can't do it any more, and without a pension it'll be worse, and things are bad enough already, and we have a little girl, you know, me and Maria, and this year she's taking her matriculation . . ."

"Yes, yes, I understand, but you've got to see my point of view as well. Our organization is already much criticized, and if I give you your pension now, just like that, without a reason, you can imagine what the unions will say, and your colleagues – there'll be an outcry! If I let you go just because 'you forget everything', as you say, my dear Contin, why, the next on the list will be in here asking for his pension because he feels the cold – it's a question of justice, don't you see? Personally, I'm sorry, I truly am. I too have a son who's taking his matriculation this year, but I'm not asking for my pension just because of that. Now, my dear Contin, you get back to work and leave me to get on with mine."

"Oh well then, if there's no way round it, let's hope we don't die first, damn it."

"That's right, Contin, let's hope we don't die first. We can any of us die at any moment, can't we? Today, a tile on the head, tomorrow, a foot in the canal . . ."

"I've already put a foot in the canal! If you want, I can find the gondolier to bear me out."

"Are you pulling my leg, Contin? First you say you've lost your memory, then you say you can find the gondolier? Let's forget it, Contin. I already know all about your lapses of memory. Go back to your desk, you've never over-strained yourself anyway. I'm not asking you to go to war, am I? I'm asking you to go back and sit where you have sat for the last fourteen years, doing precious else but keep the seat warm. Off you go, Contin, before I lose my temper."

Pietro got to his feet and left the boss's office, closing the door behind him. In the next room, about a quarter of the size of the one he'd just left, sat four girls banging away at typewriters. Another door opened off this little room and beyond that was the labyrinth in which, somewhere, was Pietro's desk. He went up to one of the girls and whispered to her, "Could you kindly take me to the Identity Card Office, please?"

The girl led him through the various offices and was about to show him the way to the part of his office reserved for the general public when Pietro recognized his own desk and went to sit down.

"Here we are. Many thanks, I've made it," he said happily.

"But you can't sit there. That's an official's desk. The public have to stay the other side of the counter."

"Don't worry, don't worry. I am the official, isn't that right, girls?"

He called over to the two girls who sat giggling as they'd done the day before.

"Yes, that's our Signor Contin."

The other girl stood thunderstruck for a moment, then turned to go back to her office.

"Miss, Miss," Pietro called her back, "come here a moment would you? I want to ask you another favour, if it's not too much."

The girl came over to Pietro. He beckoned her to come closer, and whispered in her ear, "I'm sorry, but it's something confidential. Don't say anything to the boss, will you, please? He's already got it in for me. You won't tell anyone, will you, please, that I've become such an old fool?"

9

During the brief period of Luca's illness, the sweep of blue sky outside the window, broken by a stray cloud or two, the whiteness of the walls, the pain and physical exhaustion and a general feeling of oppression associated with Nina had come and gone in the confusion before his eyes and in his thoughts, in a welter which somehow forged a shape in the temperature of his body. Luca tried instinctively to grasp it, but the object of his thoughts moved beyond the definition he managed to give it, perception twisted free of the four notes marked on the stave and plunged again into a profound density which he was unable to fathom. Every now and then his mother brought him a cup of tea or some soup, and said a few words to him; but Luca no longer even distinguished her from those pieces of sky, of wall, of thought, amongst which a chance fragment of reality became entangled, like a fish in a net.

He would probably have shrugged off these ideas if his convalescence had not confined him to the house, and the wish to avoid the everlasting drone of words between his mother, father and sister had not forced him to isolate himself. So he went back to his sketches, thought up new themes, transcribed. And every day he swore to himself he would stop trying, he would just read and sleep. But at the most unlikely hours of the day or night the theme in his head dragged him from his bed and back to the piano, forced him to challenge the limits of his sensibility and technique. Sometimes he felt he had grasped the meaning of a chord, that its inner structure was clear to him; but the moment he tried to write it down on the stave he was conscious of having left something out. Sometimes, seduced by an elusive line of melody, he would try turning the tune the other way round, transposing it or changing the rhythm, but without success. The mysterious music of his imagination took on life only in the transpositions of the notes; the torment of their impermanence and imperfection was their only possible form. He would go back to bed exhausted, telling himself once more that he would not go on trying because that phantom was a ruthless taskmaster and would not hesitate to kill him or someone else just as long as it could wring out an instant of pain or love from the world; as long as it could extract from Luca's body its freezing life-force, leaving him empty.

And when those days were over, and there were no more phantoms and no more fevers to torment him, when his life returned to its normal, swift, run-of-the-mill course in the anonymous corridors of school and home, the boredom and banality of it struck him just as violently. Luca felt he had become two people; someone had been born in his body and had absorbed all his best resources, his few good qualities, leaving him bored and tiresome in his indifference towards tidy, ordinary everyday life. He knew that the phantom was always lurking somewhere, drinking up every moment that was worth living, condemning him to a monstrous existence. Mindless, bereft of emotion, his inner world was continuously drained by the process of creating that music. On the other hand, what proof did he have of this transformation? All he had to show for it were a few songs which didn't even express the best he had to give, but only what was there.

One afternoon, with the score under his arm, he went to see Marco. It seemed impossible to Luca that Marco or anyone else could ever understand his music, but he felt it his duty to give back to the world what he had stolen from it. Marco telephoned a singer friend of his and fixed an appointment for the following Friday to try the songs through.

On that Friday morning, Luca approached Nina. They hadn't spoken to one another for months, apart from those few words exchanged when Nina's grandmother had died, and during this time, as if she had lost control of her bodily movements, or perhaps just from sheer habit, she had found herself dogging Luca's footsteps. In the breaks between lessons, when everyone was meandering about the classrooms or queuing up at the coffee machine, she would suddenly come upon him and then excuse herself: "I didn't do it on purpose . . ." But Luca had never paid much attention and now he came up to her as if to say, "Our love is dead. Are you coming to the funeral?"

"Marco and I are going to call on a singer this evening. Do you want to come along too?"

"Yes, all right, I'll come."

"I'll meet you in Campo San Bartolomeo at five. Make sure you're there on time."

He might just as well have asked her the time, or if she wanted a knife in her guts, it wouldn't have made much difference. Those months of cold aloofness had seemed absurd to Nina, as she waited for him to say something, anything, saying to herself every so often, "How much longer is this going to last, then?" But now that Luca had invited her for the evening, all those long mornings without a word, the caesura he had imposed upon their mutual rhythm and upon the flux of emotions which had always run between them, brought a lump to her throat, and she asked herself, "Can it really go on like this?"

The singer, Daniela Varga, lived in a flat on the top floor of a very fine palazzo on the Grand Canal, near San Benedetto. As they went up the stairs, and Luca goggled at the carpets and the statues, Nina pulled at his jacket murmuring, "Are you sure this is the right place? If you ask me, they'll chuck us out."

Daniela Varga gave them a charming welcome, took them into the drawing-room and offered them drinks, keeping them amused with a light, easy flow of conversation until Marco arrived.

"Marco, darling," cried the singer as she opened the door. "I'm really cross with you! You never ring me."

"But you're always on your travels."

"No excuse! I have an answering machine."

"My dear Daniela, if I want to hear your voice on record I can do much better than that."

"Very well, you're forgiven," said the singer, and she beamed at him; this, thought Nina, as she clung to the glass she had been left holding, was rather out of place. "If she's really angry with him," she thought, "she ought not to forgive him just because he pays her a compliment."

Luca, on the other hand, liked the smile immensely; he found it elegant and subtle, and he immediately broke into a silly little laugh to compliment her, her paintings and the carpets. Nina crossed the room towards them, emanating a gauche shyness much as an alcoholic reeks of drink.

"Hi, Marco."

"Hi, Nina, how are things?"

"Fine," said Nina, struggling to overcome her embarrassment.

But as soon as the music began, with Luca at the piano,

Nina – who had been so tense up to that moment – felt herself relaxing involuntarily, almost in spite of her determination to be hostile towards everything that happened that evening.

She saw Luca in that music, naked, as he was when they were alone together. One by one she recognized each facet of his character as she had spied it out anxiously, secretly: his languid gestures, his most intimate utterances, his flights. In those words of love which the singer poured out in long sighs towards Marco, the walls and towards the world, she recognized the same words that had paused in her heart, the words of their love. But wasn't Luca ashamed? She certainly was, as if they'd been discovered in bed together.

When the six songs were over Marco looked at her, and it seemed to her that he must have understood everything, that anyone who listened to those songs would be able to plumb the depths of her heart and steal those secrets which she would never have disclosed with such abandon . . . She felt her senses melt, and smell, sight, taste, all rise in a voracious desire to be alone with him. Marco switched his gaze elsewhere, and got up to congratulate the singer, heaping her with compliments. While he talked with Daniela, Nina turned her eyes on Luca and thought: "You haven't changed, you're just the same. So why don't you want me any more?" But what could she say? A moment before, she would have wanted Marco's love, and now she wanted Luca's, though at the same time she was filled with a fierce yet undefined anger. "How strong and loyal my feelings are!" she chided herself. And then again, "How strong and loyal my feelings are," but in a different tone, deep and sad this time, because that wretched heart of hers would do as it pleased.

"Right, Luca," Marco said, when he had finished his discussion with Daniela, "if you don't mind I'll take over the accompaniment now." Marco spoke as though no one had written the music; nor had he even brought Luca into the discussion of the score with Daniela.

This time the music had a different breadth. Marco had heard it alright. A less rigid tempo left the singer with more liberty, and lent strength to the sweep of the voice rather than imprisoning it within its own. Those songs had suddenly taken form, like some castle which has been glimpsed only as a vague outline and which springs suddenly into full view, revealing the strength of its buttresses, the majesty of its towers, the intricacies of its structure.

"I must admit it sounds better . . ." said Luca, moved.

"At least he lets me sing," Daniela said taking a big breath. "You run ahead like an express train, dear boy."

Marco turned back to leafing through the score with the singer, discussing various passages, while Luca was so drunk with self-admiration it was impossible to speak to him, and he was in such a daze that he didn't even realize it. A triumph, he thought to himself. . . Marco was not congratulating him because he was too shy to do so . . . The singer was almost certainly in love with him, and wasn't looking at him so as not to reveal her overwhelming passion to the others. In any case you had to know how to play these things in such society! And Nina . . . talk about guilt! What the devil did she expect from him? He was an artist! No doubt she was also dying to tell him he was brilliant, a genius. And goodness knows what was preventing her . . .

"Where's Nina?" asked Luca, coming out of his dream world.

"What do you mean, where is she? Don't be naïve, Luca. She's right here," replied Marco, tapping the manuscript.

"Has she just rushed off like that then, without even saying goodbye?" Daniela asked, happily unaware of that knot of double meanings. Almost unconsciously Luca made a strange, awkward kind of bow, and left the room.

He walked quickly with no idea where to go, wracked with doubts which turned his vanity grotesquely inside out. The empty city appeared to him now like the wasteland of his imagination, the squalor of his vain desires. Whichever way he turned, he saw only the destruction of his own pride, the emptiness of his ambitions. "All those hours, all those kisses, every word, every look, all crushed by a handful of notes, all murdered to give life to a ghost." And while Nina was hacked to pieces by that brooding guilt, fear and confusion, Luca every so often found himself saying inadvertently, "I love you." But instantly his thoughts clustered around that "I love you," which had sprung up like a mushroom among dead leaves, almost as if to mask or obliterate what was becoming little by little more obvious to him, that Nina meant nothing to him any more. He would have liked to have wept, to have hidden his head in the sand of his misplaced feelings, so that he would no longer notice what was happening inside him. Head empty, eyes empty, ears empty, heart empty, he wandered about Venice without seeing a stone, a beast or a passer-by. Every so often, in the midst of this delirium, vanity raised its head and promised him revenge. "She'll come looking for you, asking for your love, begging your forgiveness for having left you alone tonight . . ."

It began to rain and Luca huddled against the closed doors of the church of San Tomà. The sound of the pelting rain, of the people scurrying for home, of windows being shut, came to his ears like an echo.

"Can you die like this, vanish all unawares from life as if into sleep, without suffering? Let breath and warmth abandon us like the last guests at a party we have organized so off-handedly in our own house? Offhanded, because we

148

wanted to die, not give a party, and those last breaths don't understand that they are unwanted, that they should leave as fast as possible, collecting their scarf or hat on the way, because we must go to bed, to bed and to sleep."

"Maestro, you're absolutely sodden. Come along and let me buy you a cup of hot tea."

Luca had not recognized the voice. He looked up. It was Marco, well protected from the rain in wide-brimmed hat, scarf and overcoat. They went into a nearby bar.

"A game of billiards, maestro?"

"Do stop calling me maestro. I've finished with music for good and all," said Luca irritably, picking a billiard cue off the rack.

"Carambola?"

"O.K."

They began to play in silence. While one lined up his shot the other could observe him without a meeting of eyes.

"So you've decided to give up writing music? Why's that?"

"I haven't got the courage, it's not enough, I don't know . . ."

"What do you mean you don't know? You haven't got the courage, it doesn't satisfy you . . . That's already two things you do know."

"What do you think I ought to do? Continue to pillage a life I no longer care anything for?"

"What a lot of claptrap, Luca."

"I'm telling you, the game isn't worth the candle. And don't act dumb, Marco, you know what I'm talking about – when I asked you where Nina was you pointed at the score. Have you forgotten already?"

"Your turn . . . Of course I remember, but I think you misunderstood me. Music is an artifice, Luca, it's notes; they don't necessarily signify anything."

"Your go."

"If you want to run after Nina, fair enough, but why do you think that should stop you writing music?"

"Because you have to put your heart into it. Maybe it doesn't signify a thing, as you say, but you've got to put your heart into it, and on to the paper, and personally I've only got one heart, and I want that to live with."

"Your turn. It's not much good talking. You're all snarled up – you can't distinguish between music and your life. You're going round in circles and biting your own tail. You say you don't want to write, but really you don't want to live either."

"For me, the two things are inseparable."

"You're wrong. You're just moralizing, as usual. Of course there is some relationship between the two, but it's not as simple as that, believe you me, it's a great deal more subtle. Look at it this way: one moment you want to die; the next you are playing billiards. Where's your despair now? One moment you are overcome with love and passion, you feel as if every gesture is worth a lifetime; the next, you are back among banalities. You can't keep a hold on that exact perception of reality which made you feel so alive, and you're left feeling like an idiot, kind of looking at yourself from the outside and watching the absurdity of your infatuation. I promise you it's not art which kills life. The artist, as the common generalization goes, does not commit a worse crime than other people, he's neither an exceptional being, nor is he exceptionally wicked. He is just there, like any carpenter or plumber, putting together the pieces, his knowledge and his imagination, his dreams and his experience, his utopias and his illusions, using his technique and his intelligence. Everything he thinks and feels would be nothing if he didn't try to capture it in notes, or words, or in some other sign – the very next moment would wash it all away. He reaches out from the world of things to catch the hidden currents in life, in silences, in bodies, in different epochs. Which is what we all do in attempting to live. It's the fabric, itself, the plot of life. Looked at that way, art is open to life and life to art; the two of them exchange tools and ideas like two work-mates."

"They have to steal them from each other."

"Oh come on, now. Why do they have to steal them? See what an obsessive moralist you are! Your worries about theft have nothing to do with art, believe me. Listen, Luca, if I were you, I would go back to Nina and have a good talk about it. You say you don't want to write music any more, so what are we going on about?"

"I feel so utterly drained I want to die."

"Well, don't die – don't hide yourself away like this either. Go and get on with living and you'll see, you'll write more music, because you're made that way. Now shoot, it's your go . . . There, look at that! Perfect! Perfect timing even at the billiard table, steady hand, perfect precision. Can't you see there's music in every particle of your life?"

Marco collected his overcoat, paid and went out. On his way home he thought about Luca, and was touched with a gentle melancholy. The reason why Luca had not been back to see him was perfectly clear. If Luca wanted to grow, he had to pull himself out from under Marco's influence. To the young, whose lives are swayed by orgies of sentiment, love, sensation, those sudden fleeting interests seem the most important thing of the moment, their intensity obscures all sense of perspective. To betray that moment is to betray everything – one's instinct, one's feelings – and shatter life to pieces. Only someone who has begun to sense the falli-bility of his instinct, who has already been betrayed by his senses, is forced to build his life with intelligence. For him, thought has become a necessity: to be able to wake up on a spring morning and watch the coupling of animals, and human beings, without feeling lacerated by pain, without wishing them or himself dead because he is alone on such a day. It is only intelligence, rooted in memories of his own experience, which can make him understand and smile as he looks at these lovers; which can enable him to look upon misery, poverty, outrage, and weep at them, and understand, and try to understand better, ever better, and build with ever better instruments the bluest firmament, the firmament of thought.

10

One Sunday morning, when exams were over, Nina was lying in bed listening to the bells pealing over the city.

"Do you want to come and stretch your legs, Nina? Your mother's gone to church. Shall we go and meet her?" Pietro asked, looking in at her door. Nina was ready in a trice, slipped her arm through her father's, and they went out together on to the canalside.

"What a lovely sunny day, isn't it, Dad?"

"Really lovely. We always used to come for walks around here, me and your mother, once upon a time. You didn't know that, did you? You weren't born then, so you couldn't remember it. And she was only twenty-two, and as pretty as you are now, if not prettier. She was always scared I'd give her the slip – imagine, me! Me, who couldn't believe my luck in marrying her . . . She was so much younger than me, and so pretty everyone turned to look at her in the street. The men ran after her, believe me! But I had no time for jealousy, and no reason either, praise be. Poor little Maria, you know what I did when I got back from work? – I wasn't at the Town Hall then, you know, but down at the port, breaking my back, though I didn't let on – well, she would be waiting for me at the door, all het up. 'What have you been getting up to, getting home this late?' she'd say. 'Me? Nothing,' I'd say, 'running after a piece of skirt all day, 'cos I need a new wife,' I'd say. She let me have it, I can tell you, cried, called me a son-of-a-bitch and 'Where've you been all day, away from me?' And pulling my leg, I'll be bound! Poor Maria, she never could understand that money has to be *made* – always grumbling. They were happy times, though . . ."

Nina felt slightly embarrassed by her father's chatter, and made to leave go of his arm, but Pietro squeezed her hand, and went on: "Then you arrived, and she calmed down a bit. You were a sweet little thing too, always wanting your daddy. She would get at you for one thing or another so that when I got home, my two old womenfolk both came and cried on my shoulder, one because she didn't want to eat up her nice dinner, the other because the child wouldn't eat, and she must be taught to eat, otherwise she'd die – the amount of wailing I heard in those days, Nina, you've no idea! I didn't grumble about it though – it was a fine sort of concert. I was so happy I thought I'd never have anything to grumble about again. And now look at me!"

"What have you got to grumble at? You're a handsome man, even today."

"Maybe that's so, maybe. But it's not a good way to grow old with all these bills to pay, and never enough money. But anyway, I don't want to talk to you about all that. You tell me about your Luca instead. I don't seem to have seen him around the house much these days."

"Don't tell me you mind that?"

"Can't say I do, no. He's not a bad lad, though. A bit eccentric, perhaps? Doesn't seem the type to get much work done, to tell you the truth. But then it's also true to say no one would be good enough for my little girl. But don't worry, I've no grudge against anybody . . ."

"I should hope not," said Nina, feeling irritated again. She was wearied by her father's dragging footsteps, which she had to keep pace with like a nurse, and the account of those episodes which were before her time; she could have done without them. And then, once they reached the church, that awful merry-go-round as they waited for Maria – "Good-morning. How are you keeping?" "Very well, thank you, and you?" The Sunday best, and the polite smile playing on the lips but never in the eyes, it suffocated her.

"Are we like this too?" she thought, looking at Pietro and her mother, who had come out of church with another woman and was chatting with them both.

"Pietro, do you remember Signora Vianello, who lived above Bepi at one time?"

"How are you, Signora? This is Nina. Tell the truth now. You would never have recognized her, she's grown up so much!"

Nina felt ready to scream; Maria saw it, said a hasty farewell to Signora Vianello and set off for home at her own pace. Pietro could scarcely keep up with her, but he didn't complain.

"Slow down, Mum, I'm tired out," Nina shouted to her. Her father smiled and leaned more heavily on her arm. Again Nina felt burdened with responsibilities she would rather have been without.

"Why don't I have any brothers and sisters?" she let slip.

"Just because you haven't. Don't ask silly questions," Maria answered crossly, hastening on. She wondered what Signora Vianello would think now of her family, not to mention what the other parishioners would say when they heard the embroidered account of the Contins' precipitous departure from outside the church.

Over their meal, as usual, they spoke little, and when they did it was of little import. Nina did her best to be polite and considerate, but living with her parents had by now become almost unbearable. And what was worse, now that exams were over she found herself with more time on her hands than she knew what to do with; for several days she had done absolutely nothing. So that when Luca telephoned one afternoon to propose that they visit Rome together, she said she was ready to leave at once, without a thought about love or the absence of it, without stopping to think: "wasn't it all over?" or "was it worth the effort?"

The strangeness of this shared life, which they were quite unused to, leaving them as it did without needs or desires, made them lethargic and mildly quarrelsome; as a result, the trip ended prematurely. For Nina, Luca's phone calls and proposals were like a dead cat she could not bring herself to bury or to throw in the dustbin. For want of anything better to do, she would listen to him as he transfigured the irksome memory of their holiday into a rainbow-coloured fantasy, in which they had both had tremendous fun. She let him chatter away about going to live together in Rome, and stutter words of love in which even he didn't believe.

"Let's go and live in Rome. We'll get a place in Via Margutta."

"We'd need money, Luca. Anyway, what on earth would we do in Rome, you and me?"

"What wouldn't we do! In Rome there's everything – cars, cafés, parks, the river, a mass of cinemas. What shall we do here – that's the question. This place is dead."

Nina kept her mouth shut and her thoughts to herself. Going away, Luca, leaving her family; they were all things that, for one reason or another, seemed to complicate her life. She let many days pass, bivouacked on her bed as if she were a stranger to it, listened to Luca distraitly, drifting little by little into a listless torpor wholly devoid of willpower, and thinking, in a sort of dazed defence of her apathy, that she must be tired after her exams.

The night Nina had left for Rome with Luca, Pietro had

had a strange dream. He dreamed a woman was dancing in the square, slightly tipsy, with the wind playing around her bare legs and in her hair, and her eyes half closed as if she too were dreaming in his dream. Then a policeman came on the scene, followed her for a while, and took her in his arms. But as soon as he loosened his grasp, the woman spun away, unravelling like a ball of wool, and turned into Nina. Again the policeman caught her and again she spun away, until Nina bent down a little and kissed the policeman . . . who was immediately pierced through the heart by a shaft of sunlight.

Pietro wasn't used to dreaming; he never remembered his dreams and this one he tried to forget as quickly as possible. But until Nina got back various details came to haunt him from time to time. He thought to himself that he didn't at all like that policeman and was glad he had been killed, without really knowing why. What the devil did it signify, that dream?

Finally, Pietro's last day of work dawned. Maria, who had been ticking off those last exhausting mornings on the calendar, accompanied her husband to the Town Hall so that Nina could stay in bed.

"Poor thing, she had to work so hard for her exams."

"Jolly good thing too! She must be a hive of knowledge now."

As they reached the door, Maria began to straighten his tie.

"I'm all of a dither. I can hardly believe that after two o'clock today I'll be done with work. Quick, Maria, I want to get it over with."

"Now remember, Nina will come for you at two. I'll stay at home and do you some gnocchi with gorgonzola."

"We'll have a right Roman celebration."

"'Bye then, Dad, mind you don't get up to any nonsense."

"Don't you worry, Maria. I'm not even going to pick up my pen today. Let me get along now, and I'll see you at two."

"Goodbye, Dad, see you at two."

Maria waited a moment and watched him go up the stairs. When he had climbed the first flight Pietro turned and gave her a slight wave. She waved back, and hurried off home to prepare the gnocchi.

Pietro had promised himself he would do absolutely nothing that morning. "I'll just sit there, and watch the others working."

To his great surprise he noticed that the others were slacking too – maybe they'd been skiving all these years. The two girls who had giggled so much when he had confused the creaking of the shutter with a death-rattle were on holiday, and their place had been taken by another pair of about the same age; they gossiped away about exactly the same sort of thing in almost the same voices, so that Pietro wondered if they might even be the same people, and whether he might be suffering another fit of amnesia.

Around eleven the heat became so intense that he decided to try to do some work; "Otherwise the time will never pass . . ." He kept looking at his watch, where the hours ticked by with a slowness proportionate to his impatience. Then suddenly the clerks all rose to their feet in a body and left. It was two o'clock. Pietro remained sitting at his desk, the dreadful heat of that August day weighing him down and making him feel like stone. About a quarter of an hour later he saw Nina wandering through the offices, and called to her, but the effort was so great and he felt so weak that his own voice frightened him.

"What are you doing still sitting here, Dad? Haven't you got through your work yet?"

"Yes, yes, I've finished," Pietro replied with a great effort. "I just wanted to sit here a bit and take a look at these blasted walls I've looked at for the last fifteen years . . . Just think, not so much as a flower! Not even a word: 'Signor Contin, we are truly sorry that you are retiring, and would like to thank you for the service you have rendered over the last fifteen years . . .' Nothing of the sort, not even a line, the vermin. I bet it's that mayor, and he's offended because I want to retire. All right, all right, Mr Mayor. If you had a daughter as pretty as I have to marry off, you wouldn't spend your life being such a pain in the arse."

"Let's go now. Mum's waiting for us."

Pietro tried to get up from his chair, but it was too much for him, and he had to say to Nina, "Give us a hand, would you, my legs are like jelly." And as soon as he was on his feet he was overcome by a tremendous dizzy spell, which lasted an eternity, or a second – he couldn't be sure which. Probably it was only a second, because Nina hadn't noticed anything. "I can't die here, damn it," he said to himself, "let's get home to Maria."

"I can smell a faint smell of shit, Nina, can you?"

"Now you mention it, I think you're right."

"Must be this place. Let's get out of it."

While they were making their way slowly down the stairs, Pietro realized he had shit his pants. "Must have been while I was feeling dizzy," he said to himself, and thought no more about it.

Venice was crammed with tourists, people were jostling together with scarcely space to breathe, and there were long queues for both the ferry and the gondola-crossing.

"Christ, what a mob! How shall we get across, Nina?"

"Do you want to cross by the bridge?"

"The Rialto? Are you mad? I'd never make it. Know what we'll do? We'll sit down a minute out here, and wait for these bloody tourists to thin out a bit. That way we can celebrate the end of my illustrious career, too!"

"But the tourists will never thin out, you know that. They'll be milling around until two in the morning."

"Come on, Nina, just a drop of something. We'll phone your mother and tell her to keep the gnocchi warm."

"O.K, let's sit down then. You know, Dad, I can still smell that stink of shit."

"Ah, don't fuss so, for once in a lifetime it's me, my dear."

Nina looked at her father incredulously for a second then burst out laughing.

"Nina, no, don't you laugh too, it's not funny, you know. Everybody laughs at me – I must have become a right old fool."

"Poor Dad, you've dirtied yourself."

"Dirtied and wet myself, for that matter . . ."

By pushing their way through the crowd with their elbows they managed to reach a bar where a table had just been vacated and Nina was able to sit her father down.

"Signorina, we were here first, you know," said a tourist with her hair piled up in a majestic, slightly ridiculous manner.

"There's room for everybody, signora. My father is dead on his feet, he can't manage . . ."

"So what?" said the woman, patting her outlandish top-knot.

"What are you drinking, Dad?" Nina asked Pietro.

"A glass of red."

"Wait here then; I'll go in and get it and give Mum a ring as well."

Nina went into the bar. Pietro wanted to call her back but his voice wouldn't come. The woman and her friends helped themselves to all the remaining seats round the table.

"What a way to behave! We'll call the waiter and get this man to leave. He's pretending to be asleep, even! But he can't fool us. And what an unpleasant smell there is . . . Surely he hasn't shit himself has he?"

"She's coming to celebrate with us, Dad," shouted Nina as she came out of the bar.

"Surely you haven't invited your friends as well, signorina?"

"You mind your own business."

"Now I'm really going to call the waiter, you little minx! That's no way to behave."

Pietro had fallen into a doze. Nina made to put the glasses down on the table, but the woman prevented her with a peremptory gesture, leaving her standing there, glasses in hand.

"Haven't you yet understood that you must leave this instant? Waiter, waiter!"

The waiter came over and the tourist ordered, "Waiter, make this man get up and leave. We have been queuing for this table for half an hour, and this young woman presumes to barge in ahead of us. What's more, the old man stinks. Wake him up at once and turn him out or there'll be trouble . . ."

"No, ma'am, I'm not waking him, poor old devil. That's not my job."

The woman got up in a fury, and before Nina could stop her, she pushed Pietro's chair, toppling it over backwards. His head hit the pavement, and blood began oozing from his ears.

"I only just touched him," the woman shouted hysterically, shrinking away in fright.

Nina threw herself on her father's body, aghast. The crowd stumbled over them, then parted, and within seconds a ring of faces, of mutterings, was formed around them.

Nina distinguished only the voice of the woman still shouting, "I scarcely touched him, I swear it! He fell over of his own accord. What have we done, what have we done to deserve such treatment? My God, what a place! Venice! Never again!"

TWO

. . . E come il vento
Odo stormir tra queste piante . . .
GIACOMO LEOPARDI

I

The great illusion which we foster in our hearts, this insane idea of another love, a different town, of some other outcome to the situation than the one we know to be the real and necessary one – this is a siren. Those who in this world are bound to the mainmast of their fragile vessels like Ulysses are driven mad by her singing; they watch the sailors with their wax-plugged ears row steadily on, unaware of her song, and imagine that others, not we ourselves, live on that island, that some people, anyway, are permitted to seek their damnation in the siren's arms.

Suddenly one of the sailors, disobeying his captain's orders, unplugs his ears. Now no bonds restrain him, and he plunges into the sea and swims until he reaches the island whence the singing seems to come. Ulysses cries, "Untie me! Untie me! I must save him!" but the other sailors cannot understand, they cannot even hear his cries. And naturally Ulysses is not telling the truth. Were he to be freed from his bonds, all he would do would be to swim more swiftly than his sailor and, reaching the sirens, he would inevitably discover the truth of what had been foretold. He would find madness, death; or rather the evidence of that other life, the life of an oarsman or of a captain, of all that binds him to his ship.

As with Ulysses and these deaf oarsmen, we too are

pursued every day of our arduous crossing by the song of the sirens. It is a man or a woman crossing our path, news from another country, the outline of another ship out at sea bound for who knows where; it is Emma's dream of marrying her doctor under cover of night, by the light of torches. And as we have not had the good fortune to hear the prophecy – we were distracted for a moment perhaps, or are simply sailors fated to deafness – almost unceasingly we pursue that song. When we have crossed the little stretch of sea that separates our vessel from the island, we start frantically to search out the singer. Nothing. The island is deserted. No sign of a siren, not a mouse stirring. Only some stones, a little salt upon the sand; the song is no longer to be heard. By good fortune we are good swimmers and the ship is moving slowly. The sea is calm, and we start the swim back to her.

Then again, suddenly, while we are in the sea, we hear the song; it no longer comes from that island but from another one, closer by. Without a second thought we start to swim towards it, but this time realize we are wrong before we even reach the island – it is not that island but another, and then another, and yet another one again. By now all the sailors are in the water, and one of them has slyly untied the captain too; Ulysses is with them now as they swim hither and thither. The ship is empty, drifting slowly on among them, borne along by the current. One after another Ulysses and sailors begin to drown; perhaps only the last of them, gazing after the ship now lost to them, manages to catch sight, on the tedious, unchanging deck – of the siren singing.

Where, then, have we been? And pursuing what? We have pursued an echo, the intangible echo of our own song. But then, who could ever tell this tale if not one of those drowning mariners? Maybe the maddest of them, the one who is clinging to a log or a sponge, convinced that he is safe, unaware that the sponge is absorbing water, that the log is drifting out to sea, that a tidal-wave of vast dimensions is about to sweep him away, with his hand-holds, the ship, the islands, even the song! One could even say, "Would that we had never sung, never produced that echo." Certainly, had we not been born to some destiny or other, we never would have drowned.

2

Michele Scarpa had regained his post as teacher at the school, though this did not leave him overjoyed: Marina, having bought a thesis, had at last obtained her degree and, what was more, a much more important position in the Party than that of her husband. There was talk now of a prestigious appointment, even an election to the City Council. What was chiefly demanded of her, however, was that she write a book, or even better, some articles – on Poetry, Economics, Astrology, Dietetics – any little oddment which would enable the Party to present her on their lists as: *Dottoressa Marina Dondini-Scarpa, well known for her publications on yeast-fungus, who has lately joined the ranks of the Party.* Her rapid rise in the Party was due to quite other talents, but to publicize these was not considered advantageous to her political career.

Her thesis had been written by a young revolutionary student who had not fallen prey to her charms, and it was not therefore possible to use it as the fledgeling *Dottoressa*'s first publication. Instead, the thesis Michele had written for his degree was exhumed from a cupboard in the cellar and put to use. It was a work on Ugo Foscolo entitled 'Thanatos and Immortality in Foscolo'.

"An original and careful study," the local literary critic hailed it in his article on the culture page of the newspaper.

(He was a colleague of Bortoletti's who had also clambered rapidly into the Party boat, and who had obtained his job on the paper through it.) The thesis was in fact an extremely boring piece of work, its scanty ideas set forth in an excessively academic, sleep-inducing style. But by the second page almost everybody felt ready to pass judgment, thus avoiding any build-up of undue animosity against the author, with its consequent effects, as they waded through his cryptic sophistry.

Now Marina was pressing Michele to repeat the success with a new work. This time, he would actually be allowed to sign it himself. She would be content with being cited among the sources, and perhaps quoted here and there in an affectionate footnote or so. "Having read this passage, my wife, Dottoressa Marina Dondini-Scarpa, whose inestimable work on Ugo Foscolo has already been mentioned, was able to enlighten me on various points; which from now on I will refer to using the abbreviation, N.b.m.w., D.M.D-S. (Note by my wife, Dottoressa Marina Dondini-Scarpa.) I shall never be able to repay her for the loving attention and unceasing vigilance with which she has guided my hand through this dark wood."

She made herself such an incredible nuisance about it that in the end she succeeded in getting her way, despite the deep repugnance Michele had felt for books ever since his university days. The new work was entitled: 'The Magma, i.e., the People's Disillusionment with the Literature of the Bourgeoisie'. And here, the significance of that 'i.e.' completely eluded even the most astute of critics, i.e. those most loyal to the Party. Again, that critic threw a banner headline right across the culture page of the local paper: "Astounding discovery! Literature as Disillusionment."

These two works, published within a couple of months of each other, established the couple's reputation. By now the café group was small fry to them, and they spoke of Rome, of getting closer to the heart of the Party, of setting foot on the first rungs of national fame. Love between them flourished again – the thieves who came and went through their bed (the real powerhouse of their careers) no longer offended Michele, who had decided he neither wanted to suffer nor to appear a fool. Indeed, a great understanding transcends such trifles. And what was more, a reconciliation with his literary-critical-and-so-forth vocation had been of service to Michele: he now actually read the preface, and sometimes even a page or two, of the books he cited at every turn in his writings. The one last shackle holding him back was teaching: those infernal young brats were alone in doubting his greatness. Marina didn't doubt it, the Party didn't doubt it, nor was it doubted by the man-in-the-street, so Michele claimed – the grocer, for instance, who celebrated his visits personally slicing him his ham and mortadella with his own inimitable adroitness (or so it seemed to Michele), and who above all addressed him most fulsomely, with a touching sense of Scarpa's social standing.

"Good evening, Professor. All well with you I trust?"

"Absolutely fine, Bepi. I have just started to turn my hand to a vast new field of research. The relationship of Vienna to the French in 1922. The date is irrelevant, of course. In fact I intend to cover the whole period of Vienna's relationship with the French since 1492 – a key date, you know, vitally important."

"Bravo, sir! I, too, have some notion of writing, once I can get this shop off my hands. Would the Vienna of 1922 be a very difficult subject then?"

"Ehem, well . . . I shouldn't really recommend it – it's not a subject for beginners. Why don't you tackle the Fall of Rome in 1852 . . . No, don't take the skin off."

"1852, Professor? 1870, surely?"

"Yes of course it's 1870, everybody knows that. But if you don't start with 1852 you won't make head nor tail of the subject. What do I owe you?"

So, why should he doubt himself? Certainly that was the world everybody lived in; at the top of the mast the smart-arses, and then nearer the base of the pyramid, the dumb-clucks. No. To doubt would be fatal; he must aim for the top, and right now.

As if this illusory and completely superficial rebirth of self-confidence (which was in fact to make no perceptible difference to this character's psychological make-up) were really and truly some significant transformation, it seemed to Michele that the whole world was confirming this second flowering: everyone admired him, everyone respected him and credited him with merits and abilities which quite frankly he couldn't see in himself.

"Maybe it is enough just to believe," he said to himself, delighted but a little dazed; "I believe I have become an essayist, therefore everyone else believes it too." And, drunk with his rapid rise in the estimation of his fellow citizens, he invented new titles for future works every day, and it was only his extremely limited horizon which saved him from venturing into branches of learning other than his own field – or to be precise, the Magma; as literature of course. There was not a cine-club, salon or grocery store where he was not invited to express an opinion on whatever topic happened to be under discussion.

"I see you have not been wasting any time, my dear Scarpa," the headmaster said to him at the beginning of term, with a cordial smile. "You see how right I was – a little rest has done you the world of good."

"Yes, you were perfectly right. And I might as well tell you I am not at all happy about being back here, now that I have so very many calls on my time . . ."

"No, really? My dear Scarpa, you are too devoted to teaching to be able to give it up just like that. I can tell you have a true vocation! Nevertheless, if you need time off just say – you will find the school knows how to stretch a point when it comes to making room for its most prestigious members . . . Incidentally, I hope you will bring your wife to dine with us one of these evenings. She too is very well spoken of in the best circles in town. I hear she has published a work on Foscolo, who, if I am not mistaken, is also one of your specializations. Are you still working on him?"

"No. Begging his pardon, I am preparing a work on Vienna."

"Hnn, hnn, hnn," laughed the headmaster through his nose. "Always the humorist, our Scarpa. Now, don't forget that invitation to dine – any night you like, just let me know beforehand. I have my little engagements too, you know! Please remember me to your wife."

3

One evening Nina laid the table for three. Maria came into the kitchen, took the third plate and replaced it in the dresser, put the knife and fork in one drawer, the napkin in another. Nina followed her mother's slow movements, mortified by her own absent-mindedness. She saw again, in those gestures, the same restrained concentration of that terrible morning when Maria, finding herself engulfed in that throng of voices crying *Shall we call a doctor? – No, he's dead – But how did it happen? – Look at all the blood! – I scarcely touched him – Is he dead? – He's dead all right,* had searched for Pietro's face among the people seated outside the bar, then pushed her way through the goggling crowd to investigate more closely, and had bent over him, caressed his head and adjusted his tie, with the same hopeless, simple gesture with which she used to calm his fear every morning as he set off to get lost among people who laughed at him.

Nina, even now, saw her mother's bewildered sorrow among that crowd, as for perhaps the millionth time she attempted to shut the memory of Pietro away in a drawer, with a plate, a fork, closing her eyes and heart to the present as it continued to tender its sequence of little things to be done; she leaned on that flow of things to do as a blind man leans on his stick, in order not to stay frozen among the echoes of those voices, in order to quell those silent tears; and she busied herself with anything, anything at all.

They ate in silence as usual. Nina occasionally tried to start up some kind of conversation, to create a bridge of words that would keep the path open. Maria answered with a half-smile, a yes or a no, which made it plain that she hadn't heard a word of it. Only when the meal was over, after using a tooth-pick on her teeth for a while, did Maria escape for a moment from those voices ringing in her head, and look Nina straight in the eye.

"Your mind's in a whirl, my little Nina, you laid a place for Pietro, you poor thing. I get all muddle-headed too, you know, at night in that big bed. I wake up and reach out to him, and I ask myself, '*Now* where's he gone to at this hour, the silly old thing!' You wouldn't keep me company, would you, just till I've got used to it?"

So Nina started to share her mother's bed, to catch hold of that hand which crept out in the night, to kiss it and to calm it. Little by little even Maria would get used to it, she would learn no longer to expect anyone to come home in the evening.

Apart from this, Nina scarcely felt the death of her father. He had been missing from her days for so long that his absence was no new thing in her life. As she helped her mother to clear out cupboards, she realized with some embarrassment that she felt nothing, that her father had ended up in a room at the end of some distant corridor in her mind, as if the separation had not yet had time to mature, and had been put off until later.

After a few weeks Nina went back to her own bed to sleep. Meanwhile she had got hold of some university prospectuses, but she didn't have the heart to say anything about it yet to her mother. It was Maria who spoke up, after she had received the first instalment of Pietro's pension.

"Nina, we're not going to be able to manage on this. Isn't that Luca of yours ever going to marry you?"

"It hasn't even entered our heads, at least for the moment."

"What's going to happen then? At your age I was already well and truly married."

"Well, what are you driving at, Mum?"

"I want to see you set up – I don't understand what you're waiting for."

Nina found a job as an assistant in a dress shop near San Zaccharia. She felt that if she could put some money by she would be able to go and live somewhere far away, study Italian, perhaps, in some lovely city in Tuscany. Maybe she would be able to go to America. Or become an actress. Or a photographer. These half-hopes lay stowed away in her mind and didn't move from there, so that when Nina plucked them out to reconsider them, she already knew the pros and cons, and waited for them to roll across the table like so many billiard balls into the pocket of her indecision.

Every evening on her way back from work, she would stop for a moment between the two granite monoliths, Marco and Todaro, which overlook the lagoon from the Piazzetta di San Marco. From here she would look out over the islands, and sometimes watch a ship heading slowly out to sea. She would indulge in memories of Rome, which she had seen so briefly with Luca between one quarrel and the next: the gardens of the Villa Medici, Trinità dei Monti, St Peter's . . . But these places were too conventional to be inspiring, so she let her mind dwell on the tiny, anonymous streets through which they had wandered; and she tried to remember details and impressions. And she thought about Florence and Bologna, seen only from the train. She imagined some city without winter, where the sun would wake her every day, and whisper with the last rays of evening among the plane trees bordering some riverside. She watched the stern of her ship disappearing behind the headland of Sant' Elena, and the names of a multitude of distant cities came into her head, and while the foreign sound of their names rang in her ears like a song full of open spaces and freedom, a light breeze lifted her out of her own life into imagined voyages, encounters, adventures.

Supper-time came; they switched off the sky and made evening. Her thoughts remained out there among the ships at sea, or on the line of the horizon where she had glimpsed the harbour mouth, the port where she had grown up. She made her way home, sat down at table with Maria, and they ate their food in silence. Afterwards, in an armchair or in bed, she would try to read. But her imagination during these days prevented even this, as it called her away and away into those daydreams, to that enchanted future where the liners only set sail and never come to anchor.

4

For Avvocato Brandi, music was the most futile and frivolous thing in the world. This prejudice sprang in the first place from the various stories he had heard about the dissolute lives of artists, and secondly from the fact that listening to music always distracted him from the responsible job that he had in hand. Thus, for him, it was merely a pastime. In his view of the world there was only one branch of knowledge which got down to brass tacks, and that was history. Here, top places were accorded to Caesar and Napoleon, followed by Suetonius and Machiavelli, then, well down the scale, a host of others whose names often eluded him. This hierarchy accurately reflected the position which these figures had held in public life: first the commanders, then secretaries and courtiers, and after that everyone else – scholars, traders, the plebs. He had never read a book written by a woman, while Mozart, Stendhal and Kafka (Luca's heroes during his adolescence) meant nothing to him, and he wished it to remain that way.

When Luca had started to talk of a music course in the arts faculty of a city a long way from Venice, and suggested the possibility of enrolling there, his father was as surprised as he would have been if his son had decided to enter a convent of Ursuline nuns. He had always had an inkling that Luca was different from him, due to Luca's scant enthusiasm for the State and his unfortunate taste for those melancholy rhymers whose lives were curtailed by horrendous diseases, and whom he had always been careful to steer clear of in his reading. Luca would never make a good lawyer, that was obvious, but there were many other serious professions – engineer, doctor, tycoon. Anyway, why go rushing off somewhere miles from Venice, when there was ample opportunity to continue his studies closer to home? "Think it over carefully," he would say with a shake of the head every time they bumped into each other in the corridor.

During the summer Luca had gone off as casual labour to pick fruit. Every morning as he climbed his ladder, blowing on his stiff fingers, he glanced horrified at the future and tried to understand what it was he wanted to do with his life. He remembered his father's words, "Think it over carefully," but the possible choices seemed really very limited: either he tried to become what he felt he already was, or he could forget about it.

Every morning around ten o'clock the owner's daughter came out of the house and went off to do the shopping. The farmhands and casual workers, hidden among the foliage, whispered the most unlikely tales about her: according to one of these anonymous voices, the girl's name was Donata, and the previous summer she had had a hundred and nine different lovers in a single week. A second voice declared she was instead called Viola, and that she intended to take the veil; yet another had it that her name was Margherita, that she was frigid and was actually a terrorist in hiding. When there was a story that particularly amused a whole tree, one of the workers would move to a neighbouring tree and pass it on, so that the story made the rounds of the entire orchard. Sometimes, in the evening, when they all returned to sleep in the dormitory, exhausted by the day's work, there was still someone wanting to tell the tale, searching for a workmate who had not heard it.

Perched at the top of his ladder, Luca often tried to imagine what possible musical form he could give to those voices issuing from the trees, repeating the same theme in an infinite series of variations, rising over the orchard until they lost themselves in the pianissimo of the evening, then coming to life again for an instant, rapid and mezzoforte, in the restive, ironical tones of the trombone which repeats what everybody already knows. And would he ever succeed in portraying in music how that simple event – a young girl getting into her car halfway through the morning – was elaborated and revised, not according to the criteria of verisimilitude, but according to other far more needful ones which could lend shape to the erotic tensions, the social aspirations, the fears, the visions of that little group, and by so doing, made them into a people of their own?

The true identity of the girl didn't interest anyone. This Luca discovered one day when the owner asked him to help her carry in some packages. As he followed her along the passages of the Big House, he made a mental note of every detail in order to get a clearer picture of her. In her bedroom he noticed a portrait of Che Guevara, a map, a few cheap necklaces on the dressing-table and some books on the bed. Before he left the house he asked, "What's your name?"

"Federica."

Luca stayed not a second longer. He fled towards the trees, already savouring the moment when he would impart this precious piece of information.

"She's called Federica," he announced solemnly from among the leaves. He waited anxiously for questions to follow, questions which he would have no way of answering. Instead, to his surprise, his companions suddenly came over all political and told him that he was not a servant and

181

should refuse to carry those parcels. Let the bosses carry their own parcels!

"What, let a chance like that slip through my fingers?" Luca exclaimed in amazement. And again they flattened him with their monotonous sermon. To them it was of absolutely no interest what the bosses thought or did; even less did they care what that female's name was: they were paid to pick the apples and that was all.

For the rest of that day nobody spoke to him. And it was this sudden coldness which helped Luca to understand where his mistake had lain. "It's all nonsense, saying they couldn't care less. We've been talking about nothing else for three weeks," he thought to himself, mentally running through the stories they had made up in inventing that girl, that place, the world. But how superior the prolific imagination of their stories had been to the few, poor, terribly ordinary little trifles he had seen in that room; whatever name she'd had, it would have seemed common, since they had exalted her to the place of demi-goddess; a symbol of love and of social advancement. He had destroyed the myth, interfered with that whole fantastic construction they had pieced together, ruined their alliance.

That evening he plucked up courage, and as they were making their way in silence back to the dormitory, he said with a laugh, "What I told you this morning was a load of rubbish. I haven't found out her name – just wanted to show off. If you'd have let me go on I'd have said I'd gone to bed with her into the bargain . . ."

"Luca, you lying numbskull!" – "No one believed a word in any case" – "What did I tell you, Toni? Load of crap" – "She's called Viola, lads, and her father told me she wants to be a nun" – "What d'you mean, Viola? She's called Donata!"

Luca listened to the tales which had begun to spin themselves anew, and joined in as if he too believed the lies he was telling. And for the first time he saw plainly that what we understand about a group, or about a person, is exactly what separates and shuts us off from them.

No sooner was he back in Venice than all he could think of was to get away again: get away, get away, get away, as if now the only cure for his fever was a train. Among his polite, pleasant family, he moved like a caged beast, baring his fangs at their unabating kindness, threatening riot and slaughter at the merest mention of the future: speaking for himself, he asserted, there *was* no future, he would soon be dead anyway. But the courtesy and reasonableness which Luca and Silvia's parents had instilled in them stood all four in good stead during those difficult days, and no lasting harm was done. At table various topics were discussed with perfect politeness. But then the subject of Luca's departure would come up again, and of what he was going to do with his life.

"It's not true that I don't know what I'm doing," he said to his father one evening. "It's that I want different things."

"Let's hear what it is you want, then."

"A better world," Luca answered, a bit at random. He watched a tender, surprised smile come into his father's eyes.

"But you have to take the world as you find it."

"I can at least choose to live in a different world from yours."

Luca got up from the table, pushed in his chair and took his plate to the sink. He looked again into his father's puzzled, incredulous eyes.

"It's better if I leave right now," Luca blurted out.

"What? Without even packing?" his mother broke in.

"That'll only take me a second."

In no time at all Luca came back into the kitchen with a

half-empty bag, and kissed his mother on the forehead. She sat rigid in her chair.

"Hold on a minute, take this." His father had risen to his feet and stood facing him, a few banknotes in his hand. He thrust the money into Luca's jacket pocket, and gave him a hug.

Luca suddenly thought of the eleventh son in a story of Kafka's: "Sometimes he would look at me almost as if he wanted to say, 'I'll take you with me, Dad.' Then I would think, 'You would be the last person I'd entrust myself to.' And then his eyes would seem to say, 'Would that I might be that last!'" Luca wanted to say something, but all that had come into his head was that exceptionally inappropriate passage.

"Good luck, Luca," his father whispered affectionately in his ear.

"You too, Dad," Luca answered, caressing him on the nape of the neck.

He hurried out on to the landing, his mother following on his heels with a hand on his back as if to guide him safely through the doors, without, as usually happened, banging into them. And as if in these confused movements, she might be able to steal a last embrace. "But where are you going?" she blurted out when Luca was already down the first flight of stairs. He looked up at her, dumbly. Between them there was something hard and painful, a taut rope which was already beginning to fray in the middle. One moment more and it would snap, and they would fall away from one another. But suddenly his mother's expression softened, she leant over the banisters and asked, "Your music. Have you taken your music?"

"Yes," Luca answered quietly.

"So you've got everything."

Luca smiled at her, nodded, and went on down the stairs,

while his mother watched him, holding her breath, forcing her tears into a goodbye.

Once on the canalside Luca looked up at the sky. The wind had brought back the clouds, and the birds were flying low. Soon there would be a storm. He hurried on so as not to be caught in the rain.

He'd always liked leaving but this time he was aware of a strange weakness about the knees, something quaking in his gut, something breaking in him, and it was painful. It was already nostalgia. As soon as the train moved off with a jolt, he stirred out of that weakness, as if from out of sleep. Yes, yes, this had been the right thing to do! He thought absently about his days of adolescence in Venice, and those days seemed to slide away from him like rain on an asphalt road, bearing away in a mini-torrent everything that had been too long dwelt upon, emotion too deeply felt, as dead autumn leaves are carried by streams into the river, and the river bears them to the sea. Along the course of that river, which gushed from his heart and flowed back through the days, through time, Luca let himself float, while in his mind he followed notes which composed themselves into a fluid and natural order: crying, laughing, loving would no longer seem to be divided into art and life as they once had been. In both one and the other the same things lived. He watched the sky, and the nostalgia of that journey seemed to offer itself to the world in a song; and as if to a destiny, or to a new country, he let himself weep out his life in music, as birds do in their flight.

5

Marco had taken to walking at dusk along the Riva degli Schiavoni, and during the summer he had often caught sight of Nina there. He would greet her with a nod whenever she spotted him, as much as to say that he couldn't stop just then but some other time he'd be glad of a chat. This intention was only vaguely framed in his mind, to be immediately forgotten as another, more urgent, impulse came to take its place. Sometimes, however, if she had not seen him, he could watch her calmly and at length, as she sauntered between "Marco" and "Todaro", lost in some dream or some plan for her life, a faraway look in her eyes. The web of his thoughts then dissolved, as waking falls into sleep, and something drew him once more to the point of greeting her. He would return to this encounter with a pleasure he concealed even from himself, as though it was some god who escorted him to this place at this hour, some mysterious force emanating from himself, as certain tears and smiles emanate, drawing one's inner life into the realm of physical reality.

When in autumn the days began to draw in, and the fog and the cold, like invisible custodians, began again to shepherd people into their houses; when he found himself alone for long spells in those long, empty nights, the anguish of which he knew so well, the beloved vision of Nina dissolved, to reassert itself as an all too carnal absence. He looked about him for her – her smell, her arms, her voice; he tried to conjure up her presence by his desire, and fell deeper and deeper into the void of his imagination, which opened into other infinite voids where life itself was lost. And in the morning he would once more take up the everyday occupations, one corner of his mind on the anguish of the night before, anticipating the night to come with unacknowledged horror; the threat of being no longer able to extricate himself from nothingness, of being no longer able to live like others, of letting himself be drawn on by some great conviction or dragged through daily life by a host of trivial concerns. He wasn't exactly sad, wasn't even certain of his pain; if someone had telephoned or called at his door he would probably have appeared furiously normal, because nothing was happening, precisely because it was a nothingness that was happening.

Then like a word he had been hunting for a long time and found at last, out of that vapid shuffling from thought to thought, Nina appeared. He saw her in his mind's eye, strolling in the Piazzetta, and recognized in every step she took, in every movement, in every least fragment of her, something living and precious. It was as if the power that Nina had over him – that enabled him to extricate himself from his introversion and raise his eyes to beauty – had recaptured the thread of his thoughts. Just as a fisherman's needle mends the meshes of a worn net, so, by following the vision of Nina through the confusions and empty places of his mind, memories of happy days, of people he had loved, of lost illusions, all came back to settle in his heart; sometimes it was bitterness which returned; nostalgia, re- morse and regrets; sometimes these hurt; at other times they made him smile.

The hours of frustration and humiliation at the Café

Serafini, and his rancour against Scarpa, from which he thought he had managed one evening to make a painless escape, had instead survived in his heart as a stowaway. In Marco's imagination, Scarpa had been cast as the evil genius. Likewise, he had, in his mind, buried Marina beneath an excessive mound of derision. Those faults he found in her were part of the fabric of their time. They lived in him too, in everyone, and were only more apparent where the passing of a fashion revealed, through the decay of its once-accepted customs, the frailty of conformism. But he had not before now been able to cut himself loose from her, and his disillusionment had shimmered over his view of any other woman, making it impossible for him to meet or know them.

But Nina was beyond these considerations; even in his imagination he knew he could never cage her or categorize her. She was the air that bears up the wings of fantasy, the infinity of the mind. Nina had become the marvellous goal of his inner life, and gradually Marco was coming to adapt to these conditions: by holding her aloft before him, eschewing all that is mediocre, he would learn to live in that dream with the clarity of one who believes what he sees with his own eyes, and step by step to follow, with word and gesture, the beckoning of his heart's desire. Slowly, the dream grew inside his life, so that one day, without thinking about it, in the simple carrying out of what by now had become a natural gesture, he rang her doorbell, flowers in hand.

He talked and listened to her with an impatience and eagerness which kept him on the edge of his chair for the whole visit. In her face and body he recognized those lines that for so long had been engraved on his soul, like graffiti in a prison cell. He longed to caress and kiss them at once, but was afraid to see them vanish at his touch. He visited her again over the days that followed, and soon Nina witnessed in herself first the echo and then the voice of that same song; her thoughts too, like so many bewitched and vanquished sailors, began to plunge and dive again in that stretch of sea which made tangible the space and the time between them. She anticipated his visits, cherished their sweetness by tending the flowers which he gave her every day, followed his words in a state of enchantment and bewilderment. Marco had drawn out the life in her, and sometimes she was afraid he would let her fall into nothingness, or worse, that he might not understand what she was. But she too, little by little, came to look upon the process of losing herself in the things of the world – something that had at first frightened her – with all the passionate detachment of a lover. What might happen in the future (if a future existed at all) was so far from her mind that not only did she not worry about it, but such a prospect ceased to exist. One day, without anything having been decided, she followed him to his flat, as if it were just another of those natural events which constituted their lives.

Marco opened the door and ushered her in. She took off her coat and hung it on the coat-rack without looking at him, moving in her shyness with an ease that Marco could not help admiring, as when he watched the movement of a bird in the air and thought, "It flies!" For a few moments they remained in the passage, face to face. "It's all so fragile," Marco thought to himself. "We'll die of it." Yet somehow they had embraced, and he could feel the bones of her back, and her muscles tense and nervous.

"You'll have to stick me back together with glue," Nina laughed, and he too had laughed, relieved to find in her the same fear of that first touch. Then he had held on to their embrace, and waited for the loneliness to pass. Nina moved slowly, her hands spreading down his back in long, tender, melancholy caresses which slowly robbed Marco of himself.

They made love, and stayed for a long time embraced, hushed, on the liquid shore of sleep.

"Half an hour ago," Nina whispered, "I was still trying to understand who you were. Now we are so close it seems absurd not to have known." Marco gazed at her in a happy weariness. From the silence and the solitude of those last frozen winters, he felt pulses of happiness emerging, like rivulets of water that vein a drift of snow, an almost imperceptible murmur of spring. He listened as breath by breath she yielded to sleep. Without waking her he ran a finger along the line of her nose, along her brows, caressed her temples. He would have liked to make his nest in her hair, as a bird. He thought again of the nothingness into which he had fallen so often during those last years, the fear of dying, and of not being able ever to die, of being eternally consumed by an inner agony which would never come to the surface and surrender to life; that void which in a fearful vortex, with a perpetual and regular motion, had dismantled reality as death takes away life. He had clung to this dying as to an impossible love, with lacerating tenacity, letting fear haul him along in the wake of events, and drinking in the unfamiliar scents of her body, he lost himself in an enchanted wood. In Nina he saw marvellous birds, a soft-coated she-wolf, a tree in bud. Every instant shone for him as if it were a discovery. He brushed her skin with his lips, and in the gentle breathing with which she told of her sleep, he recognized the murmur of the brook which in the depths of the wood ripples down to the valley. He felt himself borne along in that current, dislodged from his own obsessions. He felt that breathing nourish him and his blood swell in his veins like a stream in spate between its banks. That these woods, these creatures and waters were all gathered together in Nina, that the mystery of life and of beauty was in her flesh and that it all hung on that light thread of breath, so frail and fine, filled him with continual wonderment, from which he roused himself by looking at her, and in looking at her, he lost himself again. The moments fled by, one after the other, into what is past and lost for ever; and that Nina each time survived their death with him filled him with a tender, ancestral gratitude, as if the very fact of feeling, which anchored him to time, were melting into eternal existence.

Nina opened her eyes, and in that blueness Marco saw the sea and the sky, already so close. He felt himself spread out towards her like a river at its delta and it seemed to him that in approaching that calm sea which sparkled there before him and gently flowed in Nina's eyes, words lost their meaning, were left bare and suspended around them like stars; and that she would remain inside him and yet outside, without his ever grasping the secret of her mysterious song; that in that sea was everything and everything was lost. He imagined falling into Nina's eyes, as when the night threw open the doors of the universe and called him to its infinite emptiness, to its infinite fear. But he was not afraid, and that infinite space was not emptiness but Nina: her lips, her name, her soul. In the half-light their eyes shone together closely, their breaths mingled, and in an embrace they touched the miracle of existence.